Terminus X

By
Matthew Gene

RISING PHOENIX PRESS

Book & Cover Design by Kalpart.
Visit www.kalpart.com

Published by Progressive Rising Phoenix Press.
www.progressiverisingphoenix.com

Printed in the U.S.A.

Book Editor: Jody Amato

ISBN: 978-1-944277-19-2

To Dad

They will not force us,
They will stop degrading us,
They will not control us,
We will be victorious.
-Muse

We are made of stardust, our whole body consists of material that has been here before the beginning of time.

— Giorgio A. Tsoukalos

Acknowledgements:

I would like to thank Amanda M. Thrasher for initially taking a chance on me and my first book, Hope. It's been an incredible journey with Progressive Rising Phoenix Press, and I can't thank her enough for all the help and guidance she has provided for me. A special thanks, goes out to my wife Kim, for her patience while I pursue my wildest thoughts, and make them unfold into another adventure. Thanks also to Kristie Vandergriff, Pam Jones, and Nancy Kocurek for taking time out of their busy schedules to review the final manuscript.

1992

Located in West Texas, just south of Odessa and roughly four hours east of El Paso, is a small town called Crane, with a population of just a little more than 3,500. Crane was a quiet town. Most boys ended up playing football for the highly recognized Crane Cranes, then went on to college, earning full-ride scholarships. Many of those that didn't were at least well on their way to finding themselves and leaving the small-town life behind to pursue other dreams. Everyone else usually ended up working at the local grain elevator, but escaping Crane was a lot harder to come by when choosing that path.

Nash Stillwater was born on February 29, 1976. He was born into poverty and was the only child of Cassi and Destry Stillwater. He was a simple boy and enjoyed being outside, always looking for new discoveries.

The family lived on a small farm two miles from town. The farm showed signs of neglect ever since the demons began haunting Nash's father again. He was an alcoholic who sure as hell didn't mind using any other drug that found its way into his hands. Whether it was a payoff or a trade of some kind, drugs or booze were always considered a valuable source for a monetary means to an end. Destry was in deep but would never admit it. He had just come off a short stint of sobriety after he'd gotten rough with a local outside a bar, which ended with the other guy in the intensive care unit. Destry had promised Cassi he'd never do it again. However, he had turned to the bottle once more, and on top of that, his wife had assumed the role of punching bag when it came to venting his anger. At the same time, Nash seemed to disappear from Destry's mind. Only Cassi took the blame for everything, and was maybe even the one to blame for having brought

Nash into the world. Now Nash was her problem, not Destry's. At least that's what it seemed.

As far as the farm, it took a dive into oblivion. Even the equipment that had once been moving and churning up the ground had been sold off for Destry's own selfish existence.

Once a week, Cassi and Nash would drive into town to buy groceries. Cassi was good friends with the store owner, and every once in a while he would set aside some extra food for them. He was aware of their situation, but out of fear for her and Nash's safety, he didn't say anything.

In May 1992, Nash was sixteen years old. When he was nine, Cassi had tried to explain to him that he had been born during a leap year, but a birthday every four years was something that he could never grasp. He never really understood, but didn't think too much of it, and at times thought it was a good way to break the ice with people he met for the first time.

Nash stood in a field next to the dirt road that led to his house, holding a hammer in one hand and a magnifying glass in the other. He loved these cloudless hot days when the sun was bright. It was the perfect weather for burning ants and other critters he might find. He was wearing a pair of cut-off denim shorts and a plain white T-shirt that had belonged to his mother. Nash wasn't a very big kid,

3

around five foot five, and thin. He wasn't the type to lift weights, and if he did, he'd probably struggle with anything over twenty pounds. He had long, stringy, brown hair that just touched the top of his shoulders and hung down over his eyes if he didn't push it back every now and then with a flick of his hand. He didn't wear shoes this time of year; there was no need to. School was out, and he wouldn't put them back on until it started up again in the fall.

He knelt and dug into the ground with the claw of the hammer. The ground wasn't very soft, so it took a few good whacks to break it up. As usual, though, he would find some unsuspecting creature wiggling its way through the rubble, trying to escape from the sunlight and burrow deeper back in the ground. He would force the claw of the hammer back in the dirt and pull hard and fast, causing more dirt to come out, along with his catch of the day. Once it was above ground, Nash would hold the magnifying glass very accurately to make a beam of light powered from the sun to burn the fucker. Nash was very good at moving the magnifying glass closer so the light would make a broader circle around the creature, which allowed it to catch its breath and cool off. But then he would move it outward again, shrinking the circle to a deadly, fine-tuned pinpoint. He would torment bugs for hours like this, all of them, of course, ending up in flames.

He continued digging, kicking up clumps of dirt, when his dad yelled. He stopped to listen.

"Get your ass back in the house!"

Nash heard the familiar sound of the squeaky screen door being opened and shut.

"That's better, and stay in there!" his dad shouted.

Nash peered through the tall grass at the house. His mom was standing in the doorway on the other side of the screen door. She was looking around, probably looking for him, hoping he hadn't seen or heard anything that had just happened. Nash saw his dad standing at the foot of the front porch, shaking his head. Then he walked away and returned to working in the garden or whatever the hell he was doing.

Nash despised his dad. He could feel the anger in him growing stronger; it was festering. He had understood what had been going on pretty early in life. As far back as he could remember, he could recall waking up in the night to the sound of his mom crying. She would have herself closed up in the bathroom or a closet so as to not wake anyone, and would be crying about the fresh wounds given to her just before Destry had passed out. Nash could remember seeing his mother's legs. They were sometimes bluish, purple, and damn near black in some parts. His dad would make sure to strike her in not-so-obvious spots to not draw attention. It seemed like every night would start the same: his dad would start drinking, begin raving about something, then continue on and on until he was blaming everyone around him. He made sure everyone knew that whatever the problem, it certainly wasn't his fault. Unfortunately, his mom was the only one who ended up catching the blunt of it all, and Nash wanted to change that. He wanted to do something about it, wanted to do something to help his mom. *She doesn't deserve to live in this shithole! She doesn't deserve this kind of life! He's beaten her time and time again, and no one even knows—except me.*

His mom had even stopped going to church in fear that someone might notice a bruise—or worse, start asking the right questions. Then she would have to give the right answers and face the reality of it all.

Nash continued to watch as his dad walked out of sight toward the side of the house, then noticed his mom again, standing at the door. He could tell she was crying. Her hand would rise to the side of her face, wiping at it. Nash felt more discouraged; something had to change.

He saw Cassi turn and walk away from the door, out of sight, back into the house. He dropped to his knees and sat quietly, picking at the end of the hammer, knocking the dirt off. Nash couldn't fight the feeling of wanting to run and never look back. He just wanted to be a kid again, to continue smashing rocks and burning bugs, then return home to eat a little dinner and fall asleep while his mom read to him. He loved her so much, and wished from time to time that it were just the two of them, alone.

He checked over his shoulder to make sure he wasn't being watched, then stood up and began walking up the dirt road. They were only about a quarter mile off the main road that came through town, and he sometimes enjoyed getting closer to watch a few cars drive past. Plus, there were a couple of huge red ant beds on the shoulder of the road that he figured might need some attention; maybe some population control might be in order.

2

When he arrived at the paved road, a big rig was on its way past. The driver gave the air horns a couple of blows, drawing the second one out longer as he sped past Nash. Nash raised his hand in acknowledgement then turned his head as the dirt from the shoulder kicked up a little bit, so he didn't get any in his eyes. He looked to his right and saw one of the red ant beds. He walked to it, and as he got closer, he could see a whole army of large, red ants milling about. It didn't even seem like there was any kind of order to these little guys, they were just constantly on the go. Every now and then, he would see an ant with something in its jaws headed toward the opening, something that needed to be taken to the mound immediately.

Nash planted his left foot in front of him and knelt on his right knee, being careful to stay far enough back to avoid getting bit. He was raising his magnifying glass into position when he heard tires screeching. He whipped his head around in fear that a passing car might be coming right at him. When he turned, he noticed a black car slowing rapidly then turning sharp to the left to avoid what looked like a coyote. The car clipped the ass-end of the coyote, which went spinning off to the right while making a yelping sound.

The car was out of control at this point. It attempted to correct itself but ended up running off the shoulder. Then it cut back to the right and crashed into a ditch that was overgrown with grass. A single, short burst was heard from the horn when it hit. A dirt cloud engulfed the car while the engine sputtered and knocked until it finally died. The car sat high-centered at a forty-five-degree angle or more, unable to back out. Nash could hear random coughs coming from inside the car. It didn't even look black anymore, more of a charcoal gray from all the dirt.

He was still in his kneeling position, but his heart was racing and his eyes were bugged out with fright. He laid the magnifying glass and the hammer down. Beads of sweat ran down into his eyes. He wiped them away like they might hurt him if they had the chance. His breathing was heavy and rapid, his mouth wide open.

The passenger's side door started opening, then fell open due to the awkward angle of the car. The passenger turned and slid out of the seat. His feet hit the ground, and the car was a lot higher than him now. Then he tried to crawl out of the ditch. Nash noticed the man was wearing what used to be a solid-black suit, but it was now very dirty. The white shirt he was wearing under the suit jacket was now dirt brown. He had a handkerchief in one hand and kept putting it to his mouth when he'd cough while trying to crawl at the same time.

Nash snapped out of it and stood up. He crossed the road to the car and offered his hand to help the man to the edge of the ditch.

"Give me your hand!" Nash said.

Cough, cough.

"C'mon. I can help you," he said as he continued to hold his hand out.

The man grabbed Nash's hand and used it to stabilize himself. "I don't think you can pull me out, kid," he said.

"Just try."

Nash was able to help him get a strong foothold, enough to crawl out. He made it to the top edge of the ditch and rolled over onto his back, now on level ground. He lay there beside Nash, trying to catch his breath.

Nash then heard the driver's door open, and could hear the other person exiting the car. The driver was now attempting to crawl out as well, and Nash offered help again.

"C'mon. You can do it. Come to me and take my hand," Nash said.

"All right, kid. I'm comin'."

Nash noticed that the second guy held his nose as blood ran between his fingers. His shirt was not only dirt brown like the other guy's, but it was dotted with blood.

"Nasty," Nash said under his breath. He held both hands out, but the man only offered his left hand while continuing to hold his nose with the other. Nash pulled for all he was worth. The man started out well, but slipped and fell on his side on the edge of the ditch, probably bruising his ribs.

"Aw shit!" the man shouted, finally letting go of his nose. He pushed against the ground with the heel of his hand, trying not to touch his bloody hand in the dirt.

Nash let go as the man rolled to his knees and crawled the rest of the way out.

"Damn, I think I might've broken a rib," the man said, looking past the gleaming sun up at Nash. "Thanks for your help. My name's Spencer, and that's Kyle."

Kyle was still sitting on the ground with both legs raised and his arms resting on his knees. He waved one hand at the wrist while smoking with the other and gave Nash a little nod. "Yeah. Thanks, kid. Thanks a lot. What's your name?"

Nash figured that Kyle was a tall man with broad shoulders. He couldn't guess his height while he was sitting on the ground, but he was sure it was over six feet. He also knew whoever messed with him was probably going to be in a world of hurt. This guy was stout.

"I'm Nash. Nash Stillwater."

"You live around here, Nash?" Spencer asked, now standing and trying to clean up his appearance—along with the blood starting to coagulate at his nostrils.

Nash gestured with his head. "I live just down that dirt road a little ways."

Kyle was pretty laid-back. He continued to sit on the ground and took another long drag from his cigarette. He was still dirty as hell from the wreck, but he made no attempt to wipe off any dirt. "What's with the hammer and the magnifying glass?" Kyle asked.

"Oh, I was about to burn a few big, red ants and make 'em wish they would've stayed home today," Nash explained.

"That's pretty cool. I used to do that too when I was about your age." Kyle looked at Spencer, who was now looking over the land. Spencer seemed a little more uptight than Kyle. He was definitely calling the shots, very serious, and to the point.

"How 'bout you, Spence? You remember takin' out a few ants in your day?" Kyle asked.

Spencer kept surveying their position then stopped on the dirt road Nash had pointed out. "Yeah, I remember taking out a lot of bugs in my day," he said very directly, almost talking to himself, but his concentration never broke from the dirt road.

Nash wasn't sure what to feel, but something about these two guys was different. It was definitely too hot to be wearing suits this time of year, or at least today. "Hey! You guys need to use a phone or anything? I mean to call for help or a friend?" Nash said.

"That'd be great, kid," Kyle said standing up, finally brushing his pants and shirt off. Little clouds of dust sprang from his clothes as his hands moved across the fabric.

Nash was right about Kyle being tall. He followed Kyle as he stood up, watching as he passed him up in height. "Wow! How tall are you?" Nash asked.

"Six four and no more."

Nash kept staring. "That's crazy."

"You ready, Spence?" Kyle asked.

Spencer nodded.

"All right guys, follow me," Nash said. He grabbed the hammer and magnifying glass and started walking home.

Spencer and Kyle walked side-by-side while they followed Nash on the dirt road toward the house. "Nash? Are you alone out here today?" Kyle asked.

Nash never looked back, just kept walking. "Are you kidding me? Me, alone? Ha! My parents are always at home," he said. "Besides, they don't have anywhere to go. We never go into town unless it's time to buy groceries or something like that."

Kyle looked over at Spencer, who had the same seriousness in his face as always and was watching Nash very close. Then he looked back at Nash. "Always home, huh? Well, that's good. It's not fun to be alone."

"Well," Nash began, "my dad's a little weird, but my mom's really good to me, so I spend most of my time with her."

"What do you mean, weird?" Kyle asked with his mouth half-cocked.

He pulled another cigarette out of his shirt pocket and dug a Zippo lighter from the right side of his slacks. His jacket now slung over one shoulder, he held it with a couple fingers. He had since rolled his shirtsleeves up a quarter of the way, displaying a few random tattoos. One was a go-go dancer with the word *Star* above it, and on the other arm were four aces fanned out and a revolver in the foreground with the words *You Lose* below it. He looked over at Spencer again, whose expression hadn't changed—very determined. He was still wearing his jacket and was beginning to sweat. A couple of beads rolled across his temple, but Spencer casually wiped them back into his hair as he walked.

Nash said, "Well, he's really the only one who leaves every now and then, and when he does, he's gone for a long time. It's when he gets home that things are weird."

"Yeah?"

"Yeah, and sometimes, he stinks bad! I don't mean he's dirty. I mean he smells like beer a lot. One time, I woke up in the night and my mom was crying about stuff. I think he had hurt her."

Kyle looked at Spencer again. This time, they locked eyes. He nodded at Kyle and turned his attention back to Nash. Kyle was disgusted and couldn't believe what he was hearing. He took one last drag of his cigarette, stopped momentarily, and pushed it into the ground with the tip of his shoe.

3

When they reached the front porch, Nash's father, Destry, had already come to the side of the house to inquire who they were and why they were with Nash. His stance was open but defensive. He looked like a gunfighter waiting for the draw. His teeth were exposed and closed tight.

"What are ya doin', Nash?" Destry asked, scanning the situation.

Both Spencer and Kyle were looking at Destry, keeping their composure. Destry wasn't sure what

17

to make of these two. They looked like two Mormon missionaries who had just had a major pileup on Interstate 20 with their bicycles, both covered in dirt, and one even had blood all down the front of his shirt and looked like he had tried to pick his nose with a fork.

Kyle reached for another cigarette, but his pocket was empty. He patted his shirt pocket, shifted his weight. "Damn."

"Oh, nothin', Dad. I was just trying to help these guys. They were in a car accident, so I told them they could use our phone to call for help."

"Did ya now?" Destry said, continuing to stare down the two strangers, anticipating something would happen.

Kyle finally spoke up. "So, uh, if it's all right with you, Mr. Stillwater, your son was kind enough to help us. Would it be okay to use your facilities to maybe wash our hands then make a call? We shouldn't be long. Then outta your hair like it never happened. Whaddaya say?" He smiled.

Spencer never changed his disgusted expression. He waited for Destry to make some sort of move.

Cassi showed up behind the screen door. "What's going on? Nash? Nash, you okay? Who are these gentlemen?" she said as she stepped out onto the porch.

"Get back in there!" Destry commanded.

Cassi hesitated then said, "No. These men look like they might need some help. I thought I heard someone say something about a car wreck. Was that you?"

Destry was dumbfounded. He looked at Cassi at the top of the porch, speaking to the two men. Kyle was listening intently to her; Spencer still watched Destry.

"Uh, yes, ma'am. That would be us. Your son here"—Kyle laid a hand upon Nash's shoulder and squeezed a little bit, indicating gratitude—"helped us out of a little mess. We're pretty thankful. You should be too. He's a keeper."

Destry's mouth hung open, ready to invite any insect that might want to take up residency.

Cassi opened the screen door. "Well, you two come right on in and make yourself at home. The phone is in the kitchen. I'll show you the way. Nash, you wanna help us?" She looked angrily at Destry. This was something she had never done before, and it surprised Destry.

"Sure! Come on, guys. It's this way." Nash started up the porch steps and Kyle followed.

Destry watched what he apparently couldn't stop.

Spencer walked toward the porch also. "Thanks," he said.

Destry suddenly didn't know what to do. He felt completely out of control for the first time in a long time. He turned and walked back to the side of the house to gather his thoughts and figure out the next move, if any.

* * *

As they climbed the steps, Spencer stopped.

Kyle and Nash looked to see Spencer drop to one knee so he could tie his shoe.

"You all right?" Kyle asked.

"Yeah, I'm good. I'll catch up."

Nash took it in stride and continued into the house. "Come on, Kyle. The phone's this way."

Kyle hesitated and waited for Spencer to look up. When he did, Spencer gave Kyle a nod indicating that all was a go. Kyle didn't show any emotion. He paused, then let the screen door close behind him. Spencer stood up and walked toward the side of the house, looking for Destry.

As he walked across the lawn, small grasshoppers randomly jumped around him, some catching a ride on his pant legs, others off in different directions, searching for a new place to perch after being disturbed. He rounded the corner of the house and reached inside his suit jacket for his gun. The grass near the edge of the house was a lot longer than the grass in the yard, and there was an old push mower that looked like it had been abandoned mid-cut; the grass on the front side of it being longer. To the left of the mower, several rows had been dug into the ground. It looked like Destry had been working on a new garden, but it still had a lot of work left before it would be fully operational.

There was one problem though. Destry was nowhere to be seen. *Where the hell are you?*

Spencer continued to walk along the side of the house, going toward the back. That's when he heard someone scream. It was a woman's scream. *Cassi.* Spencer broke into a sprint to the rear of the house and found a smaller porch with three small steps leading to the back door, which was open. He jumped over the first step, but when his foot hit the second, he slipped and came crashing down on his left knee.

Spencer yelled in pain and anger. "Fuck!"

He heard Kyle say, "No, no, no, no, no! Easy . . . easy!"

Spencer pushed himself up and stumbled through the door, tripping over Cassi's arm and almost fell again, slipping in the blood that was oozing out of her midsection. It looked like she had been stabbed somewhere in the gut, but she was lying on her stomach. She was gone.

* * *

Kyle was backed up against Nash in the kitchen. He was sandwiched between Kyle and the refrigerator. Kyle was the human shield, keeping Destry from getting to Nash. "Put the knife down! Put it down, Destry!" Kyle insisted.

Nash was not looking at the knife, but at the fucking machete his dad was wielding. "Mom! Where's my mom? Help her! Help her!" he said, crying. He was pressed hard up against the refrigerator from Kyle's weight. He couldn't break free no matter how hard he pushed. Kyle was just too big.

"Let 'im go! Give 'im to me!" Destry yelled, shaking the machete in Kyle's face. Drops of Cassi's blood fell from the machete, splashing on the kitchen floor. "I'll cut your fucking head off if you don't! Now do it!"

Nash screamed even louder. "Mom!" He pushed on Kyle's back, and had fists full of Kyle's shirt balled up tight in his grip, trying to push him off. Through his tears he could see Spencer holding something in his hand. *What is that, a gun?* He wasn't sure. It wasn't an ordinary bang-bang shoot 'em up revolver and certainly not an automatic like he found in his dad's room that one time. This thing looked like that rubber-band gun he made last summer except it was silver in color, stainless steel maybe. It was straight, with enough curve on the end for him to hold on to, and his thumb was propped up on something at the top.

"Destry." Spencer said condescendingly. "What are you doing, Destry? Your wife? Really, your own wife? Put the machete down or I'll drop you right here."

"I'm not dropping anything, fucker! You're the one that's gonna drop something, then you're gonna give me my son."

"I don't think so, Destry. We had deal and you fucked it up, remember?"

Nash's tears subsided as he listened, trying to figure out what was happening. All he could see was Spencer holding that rubber-band gun thing and pointing it at his dad, whose shoulder and the machete were the only thing visible to him. The machete seemed to flinch back and forth from Spencer to Kyle, blood slinging off now and then. Spencer didn't move at all while speaking.

Kyle broke in, still holding his hands up like he was waiting for a tackle. "Come on, Destry. Nobody wants to get hurt, all right? Just back up. Let's lay the weapon down and Spencer can do the same. We'll just calm down and talk about things."

"Bullshit! You think I'm that fucking stupid? I knew whom you two were the minute I saw you. How'd you find me? Was it that little bitch bartender? That fuckin' skank!"

"Apparently, you've got a big mouth, Destry. You didn't keep quiet, did you?" Spencer said, still keeping his sights on Destry.

"You!" Destry yelled. He pointed the machete at Spencer. "Put that thing down, lay it down, and back away from it! Do it or I'll sink this thing in your buddy here," he said, pointing back to Kyle.

Nash's heart was racing. He was still pushing against Kyle, but was now thankful that something was blocking him. *What's wrong with Dad? Is he trying to save me or hurt me?*

Spencer spoke with ease. "That's not gonna happen, Destry, and you know it. Just remember, you did this, not us. What the hell were you gonna do anyway? Run? Grab your son and run? That was your plan?"

Destry adjusted the grip of the machete in his hands while looking back and forth between Kyle and Spencer, waiting for the inevitable. "You're not taking me! You're not taking me anywhere. Not near those fuckers!" he screamed.

Nash was confused. *What's going on? What are they talking about?*

"Now, give me my son!" Destry yelled again, still watching them both.

"No," Spencer said.

Destry hesitated then lunged to his left and extended his right arm, holding the machete out, going for Kyle. Instantly, Nash felt heat on his face, and something was different, strange in the air. His hair felt full of static. The air was dry, and when he moved his head to shield his face from the heat, tiny sparks shocked him against Kyle's shirt. Then he saw the blood. It was everywhere. It looked like someone had taken a paint brush and started slinging paint. It was speckled on the walls and the floor. Spencer was still in the same position, but his dad was not visible anymore. He forced his head around Kyle's waist and saw only the machete on the floor. It too was covered in more splotches of blood, and a large pool was starting to form on the kitchen floor. He could see his dad's hand near the end of the grip. Destry was dead.

"Holy shit. What a mess, Spence," Kyle said.

Spencer was still frozen in position after vaporizing Destry from the shoulders up. Kyle finally stepped forward a bit to assess the situation, but he had forgotten about Nash still trapped behind him. Nash then saw something he had not been prepared for, and that was the fact that his own father was now missing the most important part that made him who he was. His head.

Nash screamed and ran. When he did, Kyle tried to grab his arm but missed, just pushing him off-balance a little, which caused Nash to lose control and trip over Destry's arm. Nash hit the floor and slid, striking his left knee, and burning the insides of his forearms. Spencer snapped out of it and went to Nash to gather him up. As Spencer approached, Nash saw his mother lying near the back door. He began to cry again, but this time, he was calm. He sat and stared.

"I want my mom back. I just want her back. Can you help her?" he said as he looked at Spencer. "Please don't kill me too."

Spencer crouched beside Nash and placed his hand on his shoulder. "We're not gonna kill ya, kid. We need you now."

Kyle looked at Spencer with concern as he approached, then at Nash.

Nash couldn't take it anymore and lay on the floor, balling his eyes out and screaming for his mom. "I just want her back! Why?! Why?!"

"We're really sorry, Nash. This wasn't supposed to happen," Kyle said.

Spencer and Kyle exchanged an unexpressive stare.

Nash continued to cry out for his mom, then suddenly became quiet. Spencer leaned in and checked his pulse. Nash was sweating profusely, his hair sopping wet.

"What's wrong? He okay?" Kyle asked.

"Yeah, he's all right. Looks like he might've passed out."

"What the hell are we doing, Spence? This wasn't the plan."

Spencer stood up and replaced the weapon inside his jacket. He removed a handkerchief from inside his pocket and wiped his brow. "I tell ya what we're not going to do, and that's stray too far from the original plan."

"What are you talking about?" Kyle asked. "Right about now, the boy and his mom should be dead and Destry alive. Then we were supposed to deliver him."

Spencer raised his voice as he swung his handkerchief like a conductor to a symphony, keeping in time to every sentence. "Don't tell me the fucking plan! I know the plan! But, in case you haven't noticed, the fucking plan has changed!"

"No shit," Kyle said. He kicked the ground and turned to walk away, anything to keep from looking at Spencer for the moment. He leaned against the kitchen sink, grasping both sides, and stared deep into the drain. "This is bullshit," he said under his breath.

Spencer was scanning the room, looking—searching for an answer of what to do next. His eyes found Kyle again, who was waiting for some sort of response so they could get past this and move forward.

Kyle raised his head and stared out the kitchen window. He took a breath and turned to Spencer. "All right, look." he paused. "The boy's alive. That's a fact, but there's no way I'm taking him to Terminus X." His voice began to rise, and he became more uneasy about the situation. "It isn't right, and on top of that, it could get us in a whole big bunch of horse shit!"

"Take it easy," Spencer said.

"I'm not gonna take it easy!" Kyle walked over to Spencer, stopping just in front of him. "It isn't right and you know it!"

Spencer held his hand up. "Take a deep breath. Calm down."

Kyle closed his eyes and dropped his head, exhaling heavily.

Spencer grasped Kyle's left shoulder and leaned in. "I think I might have a way to make it right."

Kyle looked up and stared into Spencer's eyes. They were almost touching noses. "How?"

Spencer smiled. "Remember Frankie and the man from Wisconsin?"

* * *

29

They moved Nash from the floor to the couch and covered him while he slept, which he did the entire time Spencer and Kyle cleaned things up. They worked like madmen for at least two hours, racing the clock. They had dug a grave in what used to be the garden, big enough for the bodies to fit in and were now standing over it. Both of their jackets were perched on top of shovels, which stood erect out of the ground from being driven down in the soft dirt. Destry and Cassi lay at the bottom of the grave, their bodies tangled together.

Kyle caught a glimpse of one of Cassi's eyes staring back at him and immediately turned his head from sickness and possibly a little guilt. He closed his eyes, still looking away. "Now what?" He rubbed the side of his mouth with his hand, soaking up a small bit of drool that was seeping out; he needed water.

Spencer watched Kyle's reaction. "Come on. Let's go get the boy now."

Kyle snapped back to reality. "We should cover the bodies first and plant the stone, right? We don't want him to see this. We don't want him to see *them* like this."

"What the hell am I thinking?" Spencer said as he rubbed his forehead. "Such an idiot. I forgot. All right. Let's cover this mess up then get the boy."

He motioned toward the grave, and as Kyle turned to get one of the shovels, Spencer threw his weight into him, knocking him into the grave. He grabbed a shovel and quickly started throwing dirt in, trying to cover Kyle up.

Kyle found himself lying on top of Cassi, staring into that one eye, and he couldn't seem to get up fast enough. He stood up, still stumbling from attempting to stand on the bodies below him, and fell against the side of the grave, grabbing at the dirt, trying to climb out. Spencer hit him hard with the shovel, trying to knock him out. Kyle winced but didn't give up. He could feel his shirt sticking to his back, wet and pasty. The blood had begun soaking into the thin fabric of his shirt. He reached high and grabbed Spencer's left leg, trying to pull him in or pull himself out, or maybe knock Spencer down. He was trying anything. He slipped on one of the bodies again, and when he did, he pulled Spencer with him, with Spencer landing on his butt and sitting on the edge of the grave. When Spencer hit, he lost his grip on the shovel and it tumbled into the grave, almost hitting Kyle.

Kyle felt like he was wrestling an alligator while holding on to Spencer's legs. Spencer seemed to be moving so much when, all of a sudden, Spencer rolled. Kyle followed him, now on the opposite end of the grave, stumbling the entire time on Mrs. Stillwater and her husband. Spencer, still outside of the grave, was trying to crawl away; Kyle remembered something. He desperately held on with his left hand, gripping Spencer's ankle, and reached down to his own right pant leg underneath the hem. There, strapped to the right side of his calf, was his savior. It was supposed to have been used on Destry, but now Spencer was going to get it. Kyle pulled at the syringe and finally got it loose. He stuck it in his mouth, biting off the protective safety tip, and turned it in his hand, holding it like an attacker with a butcher knife. Kyle raised his hand and came down hard, sinking the needle into Spencer's calf muscle. He pushed the plunger home.

Spencer cried out in pain at the same time Kyle started forcing the dense liquid into his body. The scream coming from Spencer seemed to die away before he was finished, like it stopped somewhere in the middle; the paralysis was already starting to set in. Soon, he was staring off into nowhere. His eyes were frozen in position, not on any particular thing. His mouth was still halfway open from the scream, and his hands were out in front of him stuck in a position to pull himself forward, to pull farther away from Kyle's grasp. His right hand was clinched shut full of dirt and broken blades of grass. He could see the base of the house in front of him, and could just make out the front end of the lawnmower that was to his right, but he could not turn his head. He was able to hear Kyle moving around in the grave behind him, probably trying to get out. Spencer could feel his heart beating in his chest, but it was slow and it was becoming harder to breathe. *I can't believe it. He got me; that fucker got me. I forgot I let him carry that damn syringe.*

Kyle let go of the syringe and let himself fall into a sitting position. He knew it was okay to let go; Spencer wasn't going anywhere now. He couldn't help it and fell against the wall of the grave and sat down. He didn't even want to look where or whom he was sitting on, or what part of them was up his ass; he had to catch his breath. It wasn't long before he got up the nerve to reach below him and push himself up to stand. He felt only what seemed to be an arm or leg, nothing too bad for him to block out later. He got to his feet and grabbed hold of the edge of the grave and hoisted himself up. He now lay half out of the grave, but continued to push up until he was all the way out. He stood above Spencer, looking down at him.

"Why'd you do it Spence? Huh? You were gonna take him there, weren't you?" Kyle dropped to his knees and leaned over, screaming into Spencer's right ear, "Weren't you! It didn't have to be this way! Why do you always make it about you?!"

Kyle grabbed hold of Spencer's shirt and pulled hard, rolling him over on his back. Spencer stared at the sky with two fists of grass and dirt slowly leaking out between his fingers, pouring onto his chest. The sun shone brightly, but he couldn't even blink; it wasn't long before his eyes started to water. Kyle was right above Spencer's face, speaking directly to him, looking into his eyes.

"Why do you have to be so fucking stubborn?! We bury the parents and get the hell out of here, that's all we had to do. We take the kid back to base and report what happened. Let someone above us make the next decision."

Kyle was winded; he had to stop. He turned and sat down, leaning his back against Spencer, looking down the long dirt road leading to the main interstate. "Why'd you do it?" he kept mumbling under his breath.

Spencer had so much to say, but couldn't. *You stupid shit. If you take the boy back to base, they're gonna send you to the gallows. Then they'll send the boy to Terminus X; you're such a fool. It doesn't matter. Just do it yourself. Deliver the boy, then go back to base. Save yourself some heartache and stop letting your emotions control you.* He knew it was over soon for himself. The antidote to the formula was at the base, and he couldn't imagine Kyle and him being the best of friends after this.

Kyle was finally feeling a little better. He wanted a cigarette so badly, and he kept licking his lips; he needed water, too. "All right, it's time. There's no other choice." He stood up. He looked at Spencer and exhaled deeply. "Good-bye, Spence."

He started rolling Spencer toward the grave. Spencer's hands were still in their gripped position and would cause him to make a cumbersome roll. *You crazy son of a bitch! You can't bury me; I'm still alive! Please tell me you're gonna shoot me first! Don't do this!*

When Kyle reached the edge, he paused briefly, then gave one final push.

Hey!

Spencer tumbled into the grave, landing on top of Cassi and Destry. *You fucker! How could you do this? I wouldn't even do something this cruel. You're crazy; please shoot me! I'm layin' on dead bodies, for Christ's sake!* He lay on his side, unable to look anywhere except forward, and his only view was of Cassi's wedding band. It was just a plain gold band, with several obvious signs of wear scratched into it. She probably never took it off or was not allowed to, knowing Destry.

Kyle stood up and grabbed one of the shovels that lay nearby. He scooped up the first load of soft dirt, took one more look at the bodies below, and started spreading dirt on top of them.

Holy shit, Kyle! Stop! Please! Shoot me; don't make me suffocate!

Kyle didn't stop and never looked up. He kept his eyes on the pile of soft dirt until it was all gone and back in place.

When he finished covering the grave, Kyle laid the shovel near the lawnmower, which he leaned against to catch his breath.

"Did you bury my mom?"

Kyle jumped and turned to see Nash standing by the corner of the house. "Jesus, kid! You almost gave me a heart attack."

Nash walked slow, staring at the most obvious piece of real estate that was not part of the garden anymore.

Kyle watched Nash. He had small specks of dried blood freckled across his face. Kyle felt bad for him. He started to say something about the blood, but stopped himself. "Yeah, I buried her, along with your dad."

Nash stopped at the edge and looked at Kyle. Then his eyes fell back to his parents' resting spot.

Kyle thought the silence was going to kill him.

Nash kept staring at the ground, not saying anything. He dropped to his feet and started digging at the ground, not saying anything, just digging and speeding up. With each handful of dirt, he worked faster and was beginning to moan at the same time. "Mom. Mom!" He was yelling louder each time and digging faster, slinging dirt in every direction. "Mom!!"

Kyle grabbed him by the shoulders. "Nash, stop! What are you doing?"

He continued to scream and dig, ignoring and fighting out of Kyle's grip.

"I said stop!" Kyle yelled. He put himself between Nash and the dirt, pushing Nash backward onto his back and sat on top of him.

Nash kept screaming and grabbed at Kyle's shirt, pulling, trying to do anything to fight back. He began flailing his arms about from side to side, hitting the ground on either side of him and screaming hysterically. "No! No! Mom! No!"

Kyle lost it and slapped Nash across the face, then placed his hand over Nash's mouth to muffle the screams.

Nash immediately stopped and stared back at Kyle with wide eyes, breathing heavily over the top of his hand. His hair lay in semi-wet strands randomly across his face.

"Are you gonna kill me?" Nash asked through Kyle's hand.

"No. I'm not. But, you're going to have to stop screaming and let me explain some things to you. I know you're in shock right now and that you miss your mother very much, but please, stop screaming."

"But that was the plan, right?" Nash yelled.

Kyle pushed harder with his hand. "Yeah, kid, that was the plan! Is that what you wanna hear?"

Nash's eyes grew wider.

"We were going to kill your mother and you, making your father watch the whole thing! Then you and your mom would've been in the ground together. You happy now? Does this make everything better?" Kyle screamed, keeping his hand on Nash's mouth.

Nash had stopped moving and tears swelled in his eyes.

Kyle could tell by his reaction that Nash wasn't going to scream anymore. He also knew that he probably had gone too far, he had pushed too much.

He knew Nash was scared. He sat up slowly and removed his hand from Nash's mouth. He stood up and began walking, pacing back and forth, shaking his head. He was disgusted with himself for losing his cool.

Nash was now up on his elbows, ready to move quickly if need be.

"I'm really sorry about all this. I promise I'm not the bad guy anymore; you have nothing to fear from me," Kyle said.

"I could run, you know?" Nash said, standing up and wiping the hair from his eyes.

"Yeah, you could, kid. If that's what you wanna do, then have at it. There's nothing stopping you." Kyle stepped off to the side to expose the long stretch of dirt road leading back to the interstate. Nash stared at the exit that Kyle had made and became lost in his own thoughts.

"Oh, but remember ... " Kyle began.

Nash was brought back quickly and looked at Kyle.

"I've got a gun and you wouldn't make it to the interstate. You see, Nash, there's things that you've seen now, and whether you believe me or not, I want to protect you and see if we can beat this together."

Nash was done, mentally done. He dropped into a sitting position with his legs crossed, head slumped, and began to cry.

Kyle walked over to him and knelt down on one leg. He began pulling blades of grass up as he talked and looked to the horizon.

"Nash? Your father was in deep trouble. The people that he's in trouble with, well, let's just say they're above me. They sent me and Spence out to look for him. We knew exactly where he was located, and we were supposed to take him back with us. We were instructed not to leave any family behind."

Nash had stopped crying and was listening intently, but not looking up.

"I don't know what came over me. After I got here and realized what we were really supposed to do, and after seeing what your father did to your mom and was probably going to do to you too, I wanted to save you."

Kyle shook his head and stood up, feeling that he would never get through to Nash and that all his efforts were in vain.

"Where's Spencer?" Nash said.

Kyle rubbed the back of his neck, hesitant at first. He didn't want to say too much, at least not right now. He felt like he would eventually tell Nash the whole story, even about Terminus X. There was something about this kid he couldn't shake, but he just couldn't put his finger on it.

"It turns out that old Spencer didn't care much for me either. He tried to kill me, but I ended up getting him first." Kyle's eyes were locked on the grave, staring at it while telling Nash what had happened. He gestured with his head when he said, "He's buried in there now; he's with your parents." He looked at Nash. "I hope I haven't disrespected you for putting him in there with them, but I didn't have time for anything else."

Nash didn't say anything. He looked at the grave and started to tear up again. He stopped his tears and wiped his eyes. "No! I'm not gonna cry anymore," he said, walking toward Kyle.

Kyle prepared as Nash approached, not sure what might happen. "What are you thinkin', kid?" Kyle asked.

"I'm wondering what the next move is," Nash said, looking determinedly at Kyle. He was looking at Kyle with mature eyes, more mature than Kyle would ever expect to see from someone who had just lost a loved one, especially two on the same day. For a split second, Kyle felt intimidated by the boy. Nash's gaze cut right through him.

Kyle placed his hand on Nash's shoulder and said, "Okay, okay. It's gonna be all right. You seem to have a lot of spirit, kid." Kyle walked over to the grave and Nash followed. "We have a couple of things that need to be done before we get out of here."

"Okay," Nash replied.

Kyle reached into his right front pocket and pulled out an elongated piece of stone. He held it up

41

for Nash to get a good look at it. It was smooth and solid black, but was like glass and a perfect rectangle. It was definitely not a rock that Kyle just happened to find in the front yard. This thing was man-made. It was too perfect, and only about double the size of a box of matches.

"What's that? It looks like a tiny brick," Nash said.

"It's called a Terminus stone. You may hold it if you like."

Kyle held out the brick-shaped rock for Nash to take.

"It's light. There's not really any weight to it at all," Nash said. He studied the stone intently. He even held it close to his face, trying to look in it.

"Before we leave here, Nash, we're going to place the stone on the grave," Kyle explained.

"You mean like a marker?"

"Yeah, exactly, a marker," Kyle agreed. "It's important that we leave the marker because there will be some important people who need to find it."

"What people? Who?" Nash asked.

Kyle took the Terminus stone from Nash's hands and began digging into the soft ground, close to the center of the grave. "Well, they're not the type of people who are going to be happy to see either one of us." He finished digging and placed the Terminus stone into the ground. He covered it, but left the top exposed. It was completely flush with the top of the dirt. He leaned back, sitting on his knees and looked at Nash.

"Okay, then, now comes the hard part."

"What do you mean?" Nash asked.

"Nash, when we moved your mother out here, I had to take a small sample of blood from her, just a few drops. Because your mother is buried here now, I'm going to place that small amount of blood on the Terminus stone. This will activate the stone and make it easy for the grave to be located. I have to do it. I don't have a choice."

"Okay, I believe you. Who are these people you keep referring to?"

Kyle looked back at the stone, "I promise I'll tell you soon, but right now we need to hurry and get out of here. Oh, there is one more thing," Kyle said as he reached for Nash's hand. Nash watched Kyle's hand approach but didn't, or couldn't seem to do anything. He just watched.

Kyle took Nash's hand with his left and laid it upon his own thigh. He moved his hand closer to Nash's wrist and turned it over so the palm was facing up. Nash watched, still unable to move, although his heart rate was increasing.

"What are you going to do?" he whispered.

"Nash, as you know, you were supposed to die also, and the people that are coming here expect to see that you're really dead."

Nash's forehead was beading with sweat and his breaths were rapid. Every now and then he would flex the hand that Kyle was holding down, gripping at the air.

"Since you're not really dead, though, we have to make it look that way, at least for the time being," Kyle explained.

With his right hand, Kyle produced a small pocketknife. Nash never saw him pull it from anywhere. He was so mesmerized by his own hand and what might be taking place next.

"What the hell?" Nash yelled and pulled his hand back, almost pulling Kyle over. Just as quick as Nash had been, Kyle was faster. Nash found himself on his back again with Kyle on top, and the knife was to his throat. Kyle's left hand was holding a handful of hair and he pushed the blade against Nash's throat, which was now turning red as the blood rose to the surface of his skin.

"I can't breathe! Get off of me!" Nash yelled.

"You damn right you can't breathe, so you better stop screwing around and try to trust me," Kyle explained. "Now kid, listen this time and listen good."

Nash's eyes were not full of tears this time, but more intense, listening.

"I know this is hard to do right now and hard to accept, but there are some people coming for both us. I need you to sit up and quit whining like a baby and trust me. I can get us out of here, but you're going to have to work with me to make it happen. After that we can get going and I'll explain more on the way. But until then, you do as I say. You got it?"

Nash raised his palms, showing a sign of surrender.

Kyle got off of Nash and returned to the side of the grave and knelt down. "Now, please come here and sit down," he said.

Nash did and offered his hand to Kyle again. "I'm sorry. I'm just a little freaked out by all of this and still don't know whether or not I can trust you," Nash explained.

"I don't blame you, and I would probably feel the same," Kyle said. He laid the blade of the knife on top of the pad of Nash's index finger, then looked at Nash, still holding the knife in position. Nash finally had the courage to look at Kyle.

"Nash," Kyle began. "You're about to find out that things in this world are not always what they seem."

For a brief moment, Nash's face went from frightened to inquisitive. It was at that moment that Kyle's blade moved with speed and accuracy. Nash winced at the sting the knife created, and looked down to see blood start to ooze from the small cut. Kyle held on to Nash's wrist as he tried to pull away at first.

"It's okay kid, I've got you. I just need a little bit," Kyle said as he guided Nash's hand over the top of the stone. He held the blade of the knife under Nash's finger and let the blood slowly flow on to it. Nash watched in amazement.

Kyle then lowered the knife down toward the stone, close enough to aim a drop of blood into the center of it without actually touching the stone. Kyle let go of Nash's wrist and pushed his arm back a little as to not let any more blood drop on the stone than was needed. Nash gripped his index finger between his thumb and index finger of his right hand and watched Kyle's blade.

The blood left the tip of the blade and made contact with the stone. It started making what sounded to Nash like a cooking sound, something frying in a pan, but very faint. Kyle moved quickly. He closed the knife, then reached in his shirt pocket, revealing a small vial with more blood in it.

"Mom's?" Nash asked.

Kyle carefully unscrewed the top of the vial and leaned way over on the ground just above the stone. He began tipping the vial over to pour a small amount in the same spot as Nash's blood; he wanted to mix them together. Cassi's blood rolled to the edge of the vial and paused. Kyle tried not to spill too much. Nash's heart had started beating fast again and Kyle inhaled, holding his breath, to help ease a drop out of the vial. A single drop of blood jumped from the edge and met with Nash's blood at the top of the stone. The sizzling sound was not as intense, but continued as they mixed together. Kyle slowly sat up. He was sweating and Nash could see it. He looked from Kyle to the stone, then back.

"Is that it? Now what?" Nash said, continuing to hold his finger.

"That's it, kid. Now we get out of here," Kyle said while screwing the lid back on the vial.

"Where are we gonna go? I mean, we don't even have a car; you mean just start walking? Where will we go?"

Kyle stood up and grabbed his jacket, which was still propped on top of a shovel. "Kid, you're going to have to trust me, but I can tell you this: we can't stay here."

Nash looked around. He wiped his finger on his shorts. The blood had slowed and was starting to collect at the opening. He took in the landscape around him. "I'm not sure what to think about all of this. You and Spencer showed up and now my family is gone. Who am I supposed to trust?"

Kyle nodded, agreeing with Nash. "I can't make you trust me or believe me, kid, and I certainly wouldn't blame you if you didn't. However, like I said before, you have nothing to fear from me now. I promise." He placed his hand on Nash's shoulder, looking for acceptance.

Nash was okay with it and said, "I'm ready. Let's go."

"All right," Kyle said. He put his jacket on and started walking toward the dirt road leading back to the interstate. Nash followed a few steps behind. "Hey, wait a sec!"

"What's up, kid?"

"I'm barefoot. Hang on!" He ran to the front porch and leaped over a few steps, going into the house.

Kyle waited and wondered what in the world he was really going to do. He had a half-ass plan made up, but wasn't a hundred percent yet. While Nash had been asleep earlier, he had made a call on his cell phone to make arrangements for someone to pick them up along the way. He wasn't even sure if he wanted to admit he had a cell phone after they had just asked to borrow a phone, then killed his parents.

"What the hell are you doing, Kyle?" he said under his breath. "I need a cigarette."

Nash exited the house sporting some generic type of athletic shoes that were white with a couple of royal blue stripes on the outside of each shoe. He also had a backpack with not much inside the way it was being tossed around. Kyle turned once again and started walking. Nash fell into place beside him.

"What's in the pack, kid?"

"I grabbed a couple more T-shirts, my toothbrush and toothpaste, and I also grabbed a larger T-shirt that belonged to my dad just in case you wanted to change into something with short sleeves."

"Thanks, kid, that's nice."

"Oh, and I also grabbed a couple of packs of peanut butter crackers, in case we got hungry. I hope you like them as much as I do."

"Yeah, kid, I do."

Kyle rubbed the left side of his jaw. He reached inside his mouth with his right hand and began tugging on something that seemed stuck. He pulled and kept pulling. Nash could hear small moans randomly escaping from Kyle. He removed his hand at one point, with blood dripping from his fingers, placed his hands on his knees, and a huge wad of blood-drenched spit spilled from his mouth onto the dirt between his feet.

Nash couldn't stand the sight of it, but found he couldn't look away. "What are you doing, Kyle? Are you okay?" he asked, taking a couple of steps back.

Kyle spit again and answered with a long string of drool still hanging from his bottom lip. "Yeah, I'm fine, kid, give me a few more seconds and I'll explain."

Kyle raised his hand and grabbed at the drool, slinging it away from him. He then reached inside his mouth one last time and pulled hard, groaning. Nash heard something snap like a pencil, and that's when Kyle really went to wailing. He dropped to one knee and bent farther over, almost touching his forehead to the ground, screaming in pain. Nash could see fresh blood seeping out of his mouth onto the ground. Something then caught his attention, a reflection of light coming from Kyle's hand. It was shining right in his eyes. He raised his hand to block the light and looked through his crossed fingers trying to figure out what it was.

"Is that a tooth?" Nash asked. He dropped his backpack to the ground and knelt down next to Kyle, leaning in close to his face. "Please talk to me, Kyle. Are you okay? What's going on?"

Kyle raised his head. "I was helping us get a nice head start." He held up his hand, displaying the biggest tooth Nash had ever seen.

"It is your tooth! What's wrong with it; is it rotten?" he asked while trying to look at it closely without touching it.

"It's not a real tooth, kid," Kyle said, still winded from pulling it out of his mouth. He spit again to the side, but the blood was starting to subside. Nash continued to stare at the tooth, and finally saw what Kyle wanted him to see.

On the top half of the tooth was a miniature circuit board. Along the sides of the tooth was what looked like candle wax. The circuit board had been pushed or melted down the side of the tooth into random stalks, long enough to enter into Kyle's gum line.

"Whoa," Nash said.

Kyle left the tooth on display for a few more seconds, then holding it between his index and thumb, placed it on the ground and started pushing it into the dirt. The ground wasn't very soft, so he was forced to dig a little.

He finally had it buried deep enough for his satisfaction, covered it up, and rose to his feet. He gave it a good hard kick with the heel of his shoe to press it in the ground and hopefully break it for all he cared. He didn't want anything to do with it anymore.

"What was it Kyle, really?"

Kyle looked toward the interstate and gave his mouth another cleaning with the backside of his hand. "I'll tell you all about it on the way kid. How 'bout that?"

"Yeah, okay."

They walked side by side toward the interstate. Nash's backpack swung awkwardly behind him, hung over one shoulder. Nash didn't know where they were going, and Kyle wondered how they were going to pull it off, if at all.

When they reached Interstate 392, they saw the car still nose-deep in the ground. Kyle tried to think of anything that might be in the car that he needed.

"Which way, Kyle?"

"Left. We go left," he said while staring at the car. He looked at Nash. "Let's go."

They crossed Interstate 392 to the right shoulder and headed east.

Kyle began to talk. Nash listened.

1976

The pickup was hard to steer on the highway. Destry kept a constant pull on the right side of the steering wheel. It was about six months ago that he had hit a dog, and ever since then the alignment on the truck wasn't the same. He had already bought two new tires since that day, and right before this particular trip he had rotated them.

It was the summer of 1976, and even though the Ford was pushing ten years old, Destry made sure he did all he could to take care of it. He was pretty good at playing cards and had won it fair and square from a mutual friend's uncle, named James Barger. James was the type to go rambling on for hours about how he could outwit anyone in poker, or any game for that matter. However, Destry had James figured out a long time ago, so it was James who was crying in the end.

The truck was a maroon 1967 Ford, long-bed, with baby moon hubcaps. Destry really liked it and was thrilled that he had a long-bed truck. He couldn't believe that there were actually men walking the planet who would want to own a short-bed truck. He figured there was nothing worthwhile that anyone could haul with a short-bed. Long beds were the only way to go, as far as he was concerned.

The engine purred, not a thing wrong with it. He was sick that he hadn't been able to get the alignment taken care of sooner. *Damn money. It's always something*, he thought.

He continued to keep pressure on the steering wheel. Buddy Holly's "Not Fade Away" came from the dash on his favorite oldies station as he hummed along. "Bop-bop, bop-bop, my love a-bigger than a Cadillac, I try to show it and you drive a-me back, bop-bop, bop-bop".

He was traveling from Alpine, Texas to Crane, Texas, where he'd been visiting a cousin who lived in Alpine and needed help with a new tractor that he had added to his farm. It definitely wasn't new—just new to the farm. Destry was Mr. Fixit when it came to anything with a motor in it, so of course he was the one to call when this little beauty showed up. It was a 1954 John Deere model 60. Destry couldn't believe it when he saw it. He didn't even ask his cousin Jake what he had traded for it, or worse, what he had paid for it. There was so much work to be done, and work was exactly what Destry did, all weekend. By the time he left Jake's place, the tractor was running and working like Jake needed it to. There were a few minor things that still needed to be double checked, but they weren't anything that Jake couldn't handle. Destry wrote down a few specifics for him.

Oil capacity: 8 qts

Coolant capacity:33 qts

Sparkplug gap:0.030 inches

Destry had been driving now for forty minutes of a two-hour trip. He was getting sleepy from the meal he and Jake had eaten before he hit the road. Jake had cooked up what Destry considered to be the biggest damn burgers anyone had ever seen. Jake may not have been blessed with mechanical knowledge, but he could damn sure cook on a grill. Destry had eaten way too much—burgers with the works, including extra onions, chips, and two and half beers to top it off. Jake ribbed him a few times for not being able to finish his beer, but Destry gladly showed him his middle finger in between belches, which were reminding him that his heartburn was about to kick in.

Now, out in the middle of nowhere, his heartburn was at its height, and he was trying not to run off the road. His eyes were half-shut and his grip on the steering wheel was loosening. The music continued to play, now busting out another bop-bop song. The truck started to drift to the left and Destry woke as it hit the shoulder.

"Damn!" he yelled as he pulled the steering wheel back to the right, trying hard not to overcorrect, but couldn't help it. The truck's rear swerved a couple times and the tires screeched out. "Stay awake, Destry!" he screamed to himself and started slapping his right leg with his hand. He continued talking loudly, not really saying anything, just babbling about whatever. "La la la la," he said, making up words and noises to keep himself alert. He squeezed the bridge of his nose and blinked hard, looking at the road ahead. The hash marks on the road seemed to double only briefly, then went back together as one.

"Shit, let's not do that again," he said to himself. He had this habit of talking to himself for two reasons. One, because it helped him stay awake, but for the most part, when he found himself in stressful situations, hearing his own voice helped him stay calm and more alert. He learned this when he was a child. Whether it was being afraid of the dark in his room at night or trying to avoid a bully at school by sneaking out just before the bell rang, it always seemed to work for him.

Destry pulled the truck to the side of the road, holding on carefully to the steering wheel as he eased the truck onto the shoulder. The tires gripped the rough pavement and made it increasingly harder to steer as the truck slowed. The sound that came from the tires on the grooved pavement was a low moaning that slowed and became lower in pitch as the truck's momentum decreased. The moaning made the whole truck sound like some large piece of machinery shutting down at the end of its cycle.

He finally got it stopped and threw the truck into park with an exaggerated movement. He was exhausted. When he put the truck in park, the truck's forward movement hadn't actually stopped, which made the transmission grab hold and the truck jerked hard.

Destry looked out of his driver's side window while laying his head on the steering wheel, wishing he could take a nap right then and there. He wasn't sure where he was. All he knew was that he was somewhere in between Alpine and Fort Stockton.

"All right, come on Destry," he announced. He opened the door and got out screaming. "Wake up! Wake up!"

He left the door open and continued walking toward the back of the truck. When he reached the tailgate, he turned and walked back to the front of the truck, shutting the driver's door along the way. He continued to lecture himself while now making a complete circle of the truck. "You don't have much farther to go, fucker! Keep your wits together and wake up!" He continued circling the truck, slapping his face every second or third word. "Come on, you can do this!"

He reached the rear of the truck and bent over, one hand resting on the top edge of the tailgate and the other on his knee. He took a deep breath and stood up, looking across the median toward the other side of the freeway. The sun had gone down and the sky was much darker, especially behind him. He took one last deep breath and looked to the east. When he did, he saw the very thing that he would later wish he could forget, but would stay with him the rest of his days.

At first he thought he was seeing things, maybe catching a glimpse of a shooting star. *Surely that star wasn't moving; it was me,* he thought.

He looked again and saw the same star holding steady, then move again. Destry slowly bent at the knees until he was sitting on the ground with his feet folded up neatly under him, gawking at the sky. The star would move ever so slightly and hold for as little as thirty seconds or up to a minute. It was like it was pausing, waiting for something else to happen before it was allowed to proceed, and it was getting lower with every movement. He wasn't sure how long he sat there watching—four, maybe five minutes.

The star dropped in the sky toward the ground, fast but steady. As it came down, Destry noticed the shape: it definitely wasn't a plane or helicopter of any kind, but it wasn't perfectly round, either. The darkness was messing with his eyes, creating more shadows than normal. He guessed the shape was oblong, possibly triangular, and as it lowered, it was getting bigger. Most of all, he realized, just as it went out of sight, there was no sound coming from it. He guessed it had landed or crashed, but if it was the latter, where was the smoke and the fire? He had to know.

He strained to look out across the open field, but it was too dark. He recalled that when he had driven up he had been able to see, and remembered that it had looked pretty flat. If only he could take the truck he would at least feel a little safer, but he'd be taking the chance of getting the damn thing stuck in a ditch. He walked to the edge of the shoulder where it met with the grass and strained his eyes, looking into the dark, trying to see how far away it landed—but no such luck.

"Wait a sec!" he said.

Destry went around to the driver's side of the truck, opened the door, and looked between the body of the truck and the back of the seat. There, wedged in, was his flashlight. He forgot he had brought it along on the trip in case he ended up staying later in the evening to work on Jake's tractor, *or if he felt like he might see a UFO that just happened to land off the edge of the freeway and he could check it out,* he thought.

He pushed the button and the light flickered; he gave it one good whack to the side with the palm of his hand and the light stayed on.

"All right! Now we're cookin' with gas," he said as he shut the truck's door, and walked toward the field.

As he walked, he noticed that the ground felt no different than the shoulder of the road; it too was hard, with very little substance below his feet. Using the flashlight, Destry could see small white rocks, broken twigs, and dead grass, and the field was generally made up of a mixture of wild grass and shrubs. The shrubs varied in size from just below the knee and to his waist. They were very rigid and too hard if rubbed up against. There wasn't much out here in West Texas—well, except for the rattlesnakes. This thought occurred to him at the same time he ran into the barbed-wire fence.

"Jesus!" he screamed and jumped back. "You scared the bejesus outta me!" he yelled at the fence.

"C'mon, Destry, how could you be so stupid? You know there's a barbed-wire fence out here and in every other God-forsaken field."

He knelt down and caught his breath. *Okay*, he thought and continued toward the fence, studying it, deciding a good entry point.

He found what seemed like the best spot. Out of the four strands of wire that were running from post to post, the third one from the top was sagging down, having come loose from one of the posts. Destry held the flashlight in his left hand while he poked his right leg through the opening until he found the ground on the other side. He placed his right hand through and began pushing down on the wire, very careful not to touch the barbs that stood at attention, and bent forward as far as possible without touching his chest to the wire. He began slowly moving to his right until his midsection was on the other side and stood up. Then he was able to pull his left leg through.

He started walking again, noticing lights in the distance. He couldn't make anything out, just lights moving about, some sort of activity, and beams of light shining through a patch of trees now and then. It dawned on him that if he could see those lights, someone might be able to see his.

Damn, he said to himself as he cupped the end of the flashlight. *Now what?*

He kept his hand in this position and continued to walk at a steady pace, every once in a while uncupping his hand long enough for a quick glance in front of him to see what obstacles might lie ahead. This seemed to work quite well; he could see far enough ahead, and his eyes were quickly adjusting to the dark. The taller shrubs were easy to spot, throwing large black shadows in front of him. The toughest part was watching the ground, trying to find the best spots to step. He didn't want to accidentally step in a hole and twist his ankle. He fell at least twice along the way, once actually dropping the flashlight, and it rolled up under a shrub. It seemed like a lifetime as he fetched the flashlight. He struggled, trying to cover the beacon of light signaling his exact location.

"Christ!" he said under his breath. "That hurt. You're almost there Destry, keep your head together."

He was still on the ground on his back, looking up at the sky with the flashlight safely back in his hand. He closed his eyes, took a couple more breaths, then he heard voices. His eyes popped open and held his breath, trying to listen—really trying to hear what was being said. It was someone speaking through a megaphone or loud-speaker like at a baseball game, just far enough away that he would have to stop breathing to pick up a word here or there. He thought he was going to come across some sort of drug deal, but the main reason he was out there was because of the light thingy in the sky that had crashed or landed.

"Truck five, truck five, to your position," the loudspeaker blasted, and continued something about "walkers." Destry couldn't make it out. He jumped to his feet and looked around and ran faster along the ground, crouched over with the flashlight off, doing his best not to trip over anything. The lights ahead were helping with his vision, and he was able to see what was ahead of him almost entirely. He reached a tree line, hid behind one of the bigger ones, and stopped.

The sheer size of the damn thing was incredible; it looked like a football field hovering above the ground. Destry kept thinking he knew what it really was. *There's no way that's a UFO. I've seen it before, somewhere else.*

It looked like a giant wing without the fuselage in the middle, normally separating the two; it was just fused together as one piece, making one big wing. There were lights running along the edges near the ends. He couldn't get over the color of it. Destry thought maybe silver, black, or both. It looked like a mirror, hard to see against the night sky with all the lights reflecting off it from the men and their equipment. There was a large section in the bottom that was open, but he couldn't see anything in particular except light, which was illuminating the ground beneath it. The military was everywhere. There were several generic, unmarked semi-trucks parked in a row, along with a few covered military transport vehicles, as well as a couple of stations set up with military personnel at what appeared to be checkpoints. He also noticed some non-military vehicles, probably government officials of some sort overseeing the operation. Men and women were moving about, all with someplace to be, everyone working rapidly and with coordination.

This looks like it's been done a few times, Destry thought to himself.

"Okay, truck five, ease it back," the loudspeaker announced.

Destry jumped at the sound. He looked around, trying to figure out where the announcer was located. He wasn't sure, but smiled to himself thinking he was probably the smallest guy in the company, and that was all he was good at—giving orders over a microphone.

A semi was backing up, moving closer to the wing, and positioning itself near the spotlight on the ground. The loudspeaker erupted again: "Easy, truck five, easy." The truck's movement slowed to a crawl. "Hold your position."

The truck stopped. The driver set the air brakes and turned on the hazard lights. The brakes let out a loud hiss while the dirt and dust on the ground kicked up into the air, swirling around before drifting away into the darkness.

Destry could see that the driver of the truck had already exited the cab and was walking back to the end of the trailer. He watched his feet kicking up dust as he walked. He also noticed another person coming from the opposite direction to meet up with him. This person appeared to be male and wore all black, but it didn't look like any sort of military uniform—more like a jumpsuit, as a pilot or a mechanic might wear.

When the driver reached the end, he didn't even acknowledge the other man, just opened the trailer, pushed the doors back to the sides, and secured them for unloading.

I've got it! Destry said to himself. *I know where I've seen this thing, this wing, but it's different.* He remembered watching TV one night about military strategies and old World War II footage. One of the highlighted segments of the show was the Northrop YB-49 flying wing. *The damn thing looks almost exactly like it, just bigger. A lot bigger.*

He continued to stare up at the monstrosity of a ship that seemed to hang above the ground while making no sound at all. The only sounds he could hear were random generators powering the lights, various electronics used by the military, and the idling coming from the semi-trucks waiting their turn in line. He looked back down at the truck that was backed into position and watched as someone— he guessed the driver— in the trailer, hauling what appeared to be crates to be unloaded. Destry noticed there wasn't any type of forklift on the ground to move the crates, and the guy wearing all black didn't look like much help just standing there.

The man on the ground raised his hand. He held something, and the crate lifted off the end of the trailer. It floated silently in the air moving out of the trailer. The man turned while guiding the crate to one side, clear of the truck, and set it on the ground with ease. Destry rubbed his eyes frantically. *You've gotta be shittin' me.*

He leaned in closer to the tree, hugging it with his right arm, straining a little harder to make sure he really did see what he thought he saw. The same man walked to the opposite end of the crate and raised his arm again. The crate lifted off the ground, and the man pushed it without any effort toward the light coming from underneath the ship. Destry could hear the driver struggling in the truck, probably from a palette jack from the noise he was making. Then the driver placed another crate at the back of the trailer, ready to be unloaded.

If only you had that thingamajig the other dude has, it might be easier, Destry said to himself, grinning.

The crate finally made its way into the circle of light under the ship and the man lowered his arm. The crate set down on the ground. Destry watched as the man walked back to the truck for another load, and that's when he heard a loud, but not intolerable deep tone coming from somewhere. It was a short burst of tone, after which the crate lifted off the ground and traveled up into the ship.

Well, I'll be damned. Who are these guys and how long have they been able to move things around like that? Better yet, what's in the crates?

Destry let go of the tree and made his way down the small incline to get a closer look.

"Hold it right there!"

Destry froze in his tracks. "Oh, no," he said under his breath.

"Turn around and keep your hands up," a timid voice said.

Destry could hear that whoever was at the end of that voice was scared, probably more than he was. He turned around the best he could on the side of the hill with his hands level with his shoulders, still holding his flashlight. When he looked at his would-be foe, he saw a young boy holding what looked like an M-16 by his waist, pointed right at Destry. The gun was not being held steadily; this guy was nervous, which made Destry very uncomfortable. *What if he pulls the trigger by mistake?* He wanted to make sure to be extra careful and not move at all.

"It's all right kid, I'm unarmed, please don't shoot," Destry said, but then his left foot slipped, which was lower than his right.

The kid jumped, raised his gun, and planted the butt of it in the pocket of his shoulder.

"Wait! Wait! It's okay, I slipped! Please don't shoot!" Destry yelled.

"What are you doing here?" the young soldier asked.

"I promise I'll answer any question you want to ask, but may I please walk up two or three steps to get on level ground again? I'm slipping and I don't want you to shoot me by mistake. I promise, again, I'm unarmed," Destry explained.

The soldier looked Destry up and down. "I don't know about that, sir. You are trespassing."

"I'm Destry. Destry Stillwater. What's your name, kid?"

"Mike Reynolds," he said as he adjusted the gun on his shoulder.

"Okay, Mike, now that we know each other, may I please come up to level ground?"

Mike paused. "I guess that'd be okay. Don't be tryin' any funny stuff. I was the best shot in my class."

If Destry wasn't scared earlier, he was definitely spooked now. *Shit, if he's the best, I'm glad I didn't get the worst. I'd already be dead, or I might have gotten away.* "Okay, here I come, nice and easy," Destry said.

"Okay, you promise? No sudden moves, right?"

"I promise, kid, no sudden moves. I just don't wanna fall."

"Okay, move slowly," Mike said.

Destry walked up the incline the best he could, looking down to watch his footing. Mike backed up a little, the gun shaking in his hands. He lowered it down to his waist again, looking behind him and to the sides, making sure Destry was alone. Destry slipped and fell to his hands, catching himself on the hard ground.

"Whoa, hey!" Mike yelled and stepped forward with the gun raised again. "What are you doing?"

"Stop, kid, stop! I slipped, that's all." Destry was praying frantically that he wasn't going to lose his head right there. "Please let me get up and continue; I'm almost there."

Mike took a deep breath. He could care less whether or not this guy got on level ground. What he needed to do was get his ass in gear and call for backup in case this guy turned out to be some sort of badass pretending to look like a helpless, overweight hillbilly. He had watched too many movies and didn't want to be one of those guys who had their gun taken and shot with it. "All right, hurry up!" Mike said.

Destry was really confused. He didn't want to move too fast and freak the kid out, but he didn't want to move too slowly either.

Mike continued to back up while Destry got to his feet and glanced behind with jerking movements, making sure he wasn't being ambushed. "D-19, D-19," Mike began speaking into the radio strapped to his shoulder, trying to push the button with his left hand and holding the gun with his right. The gun slipped and pointed straight down at the ground.

Destry jumped a little and raised his hands to shoulder level. Mike let go of the button, grabbed at the gun and hoisted it back into position.

Destry let out a very quiet, "Easy, kid."

Mike was able to get the gun back into position with a better grasp, squeezing the butt of the gun between his ribcage and arm. He slowly raised his left hand, finding the mic and the small button located on the side. He pressed firmly, never taking his stinging eyes off of Destry. Sweat ran down his forehead. He continued: "D-19, D-19, we have a perimeter breach in sector two; repeat, perimeter breach in sector two."

Destry couldn't believe how calmly the young soldier spoke over the radio, judging by his appearance and demeanor.

Mike dropped his hand back to the gun and looked at Destry. He quickly raised it and wiped away the sweat from his brow before placing it back at his side.

"You did good, kid."

"You did too, sir, but please don't talk," Mike said while adjusting his footing.

Destry gave a small nod and noticed Mike's eyes shift a little, looking beyond him. Something or someone was coming closer.

An awkward silence ensued while Destry stood looking at Mike or trying not to look directly at him. He felt that time had slowed, but in reality, just a few seconds had passed when he heard a combination of footsteps and soldiers speaking to one another as they came closer.

"Move! Move!" He could hear them approaching. The sound of their gear as it shifted about on their bodies and by the sound of their boots on the ground, it appeared there were several of them starting to surround him, as well as Mike. Destry could see movement in his peripheral vision, but didn't look up. He continued to stare at the ground, wishing he had kept driving. He kept wondering if he would have made it home okay, or if he would have nodded off and ended up in a ditch somewhere with his wife wondering what had happened. Right about now, he would've taken the ditch.

The sound of the men moving into position subsided and Destry slowly raised his head. He saw another soldier forcing Mike back. "Get lost, Reynolds," the soldier commanded, before placing his sights on Destry.

Destry watched as Mike cowered, lowering his gun. He walked backward out of the circle that had been formed. His eyes were full of fear and sorrow for Destry, and Destry knew it. As Destry stood there, he grew even more uncomfortable. He was now looking down the barrel of an M-16 from the other direction. He could see nothing but the tip of the barrel and one of the soldier's eyes, the other closed tight. No one made a sound. He knew they meant business, and awkwardly, he was beginning to miss his old buddy, Mike. One false move around these guys, and he could kiss his ass goodbye.

There were at least eight surrounding him, but he didn't dare look around to verify the count. At last, Destry heard a voice. "D-19, perimeter secure, repeat perimeter is secure; the bug is intact."

Bug? Destry thought. *I guess I'm the bug.*

"Copy that Rover-1, perimeter secure. Standby for intercept."

What's that supposed to mean? Intercept. Somebody's just gonna take me back to my truck, right? Destry didn't know what was going to happen next. He couldn't help but wonder if he was really going to survive this night. Were they really going to let him go? He couldn't imagine they would, but what else would they do with him? Kill him? At this point, the only real thing on his mind was his wife. It was too early for her to miss him and alert authorities; he would still be driving at this point. She wouldn't start wondering where he was for at least another hour, maybe an hour and a half. There was no way these people were letting him go. He watched someone or some *thing* levitate crates off the back of a semi and load them into a contraption that looked like a giant wing. He couldn't even tell if it was an airplane or not. He knew better than that, though. There were no wheels on the ground holding the ship up; it was floating like the crates. Even if he tried to play dumb and they bought it, he still had stumbled upon a military operation obviously not supposed to be made public. *So, what are they gonna do with me?*

Destry glanced at the ground to avoid staring at the guy behind the gun. He was deep in thought about his situation. Some movement caught his attention, and when he raised his head, he noticed several of the soldiers lowering their weapons and backing up. He heard footsteps approaching behind him. He turned his head to the left and saw someone walking past him, someone big. The tension was too high to handle.

As the person passed him, Destry uttered to himself, *Christ!* He dropped his arms and began to back up a little to make room, and not one soldier told Destry otherwise. He couldn't get over what he was seeing. This person was big. *Huge! What were they, seven foot? Seven five? This guy's at least eight feet tall!*

Destry finally noticed that the person entering this small circle of fun was the same person who had been moving the crates around. He was dressed in all black with no visible markings or insignia. Destry wasn't sure if this person was military or not. They definitely came from some branch of the government, probably the one that held all the government's secrets, the kind that even the president himself doesn't know about.

He watched as the figure stopped in front of the soldier who had had his sights on Destry a few minutes earlier. No one was even paying attention to Destry now, it seemed. He realized that with everyone watching Mr. Big, he might have been able to walk away unnoticed. Of course, he was only fooling himself. He was amazed at this rare sighting and couldn't wait for the guy to turn around. His heart raced with anticipation to see what the figure looked like. He felt he'd be pretty let down if the guy turned around and had a child-like face, baby-smooth, or something that didn't fit with the stature he sported.

Destry looked around at the soldiers. There seemed to be a sense of calm among them. There they all were, looking up at whoever this person was, almost as if they were in the presence of something more powerful than them, and yet they were completely content.

At last, the figure turned around and looked down at Destry.

When Destry was six years old, his mother and father were regular churchgoers. It was a ritual every Sunday morning. Destry's father, Robert, would wake him up by seven a.m. and help him get dressed. Then they would go to the kitchen to eat breakfast with his wife Elizabeth. They enjoyed each other's company around the breakfast table. His were very good parents; they worked hard and tried their best to mold Destry into a responsible young man so that he would mix right in with the great American melting pot. Someday, he would have his own family, and pass on what he knew to his own children. Maybe, if they were lucky enough, they would still be around to hold their grandchildren, and maybe even great-grandchildren, and know that they did well.

They had both been raised in Christian homes and believed that they should pass on the same belief system that had been taught to them. Once at church, Robert and Elizabeth would escort Destry to the Sunday school classroom to meet with the rest of the children. Then Robert and his wife would find their usual pew in the main sanctuary and visit quietly with another couple that they had befriended through the church until the service began.

Destry loved Sunday school. He liked to hear some of his favorite Bible stories, like the one where this old man named Noah built this huge boat to save his family from a flood and had collected all the animals of the world to ride with them. Destry thought it was pretty cool of that guy to save every kind of animal. He often wondered if Noah really did get every single animal. Like the mosquito—did he get that one? What about leeches? Destry didn't care for those at all. One time his dad told him not to get in the river, but he did and ended up getting a leech stuck right on his ass. After Destry pleaded with him not to do it, Robert pulled the leech off quickly. Destry never forgot that day or the pain.

There was another Bible story he thought was amazing. It was about this young man named Daniel who was trapped in a lion's den, but was not harmed at all. His dad had told him it was because God had been with Daniel throughout his life and protected him. Probably Destry's favorite story was of the creation in the book of Genesis. He found it amazing that nothing would be here at all if it had not been for God—even the light!

Destry wondered sometimes if God was with him while he played with his friends. Sometimes he talked to God while he was playing alone and really enjoyed it. He would talk to God like he was really there and share all his worries and wishes.

Destry froze when he saw the face looking down at him. He felt his bowels start to give, and he tightened up quickly. *What the hell is that?*

The face definitely belonged to a man, at least by first glance. It was not grotesque, but at the same time it was hard to not stare. It was just so different. Destry couldn't help but wonder if it was real, a mask, or a joke being played on him. He started to smile, but that faded quickly when the figure moved its facial muscles in such a way that it might have known Destry doubted the situation. The figure's eyes were planted much wider than his own, and the bridge of the nose was almost invisible, nearly flat, but continued down into a long, slender nose that was very thin. The mouth too was very small, like a single line draw on its face. To Destry, the face reminded him of an upside-down triangle.

He flashed back to everything his parents had told him about religion and the beginning of life. Everything from Sunday school and sitting in church with his parents made him question things. *Was it real? Did it happen?*

All of it ran through his mind in a whirlwind. He had always wondered if aliens were real, and he had always heard different theories about aliens creating humans through DNA experimentation. But this went against all he was taught. *What about God?* he couldn't help but wonder. *Was religion real or did God create the aliens, too?* One thing was certain: Destry was now standing in the presence of some *thing* that was not human. He was looking directly in the eyes of an alien.

The alien kept staring, although it didn't make Destry uncomfortable; he was still in awe. Destry couldn't help but feel an overbearing sense of guilt and that he needed to explain why he was there, interrupting whatever they were doing. Without thinking, he said, "I'm sorry." Immediately the feeling of guilt subsided. He felt more at ease and the alien looked at something beyond him. Destry heard more footsteps, and the sound was a relief. Someone else approached from behind. Destry looked and a familiar face was looking right back at him.

Major William Larson walked out of the brush toward Destry. When the major saw him clearly, his stern look disappeared, and he offered his hand in recognition. "Destry! What the hell are you doing out here?" he asked. The major turned back to the soldier escorting him. "Take yourself and the rest of these soldiers back to base and continue as planned. I've got this under control."

"But sir?" the soldier began.

"You don't like that idea, soldier?" the major interrupted.

The soldier swallowed hard and yelled, "Okay, bring it in! Back to base on my lead!"

All the soldiers snapped to attention, gathered themselves and their gear, and began making their way back through the brush and down the hill. A few of them gave Destry a look of disgust as they walked by, but not Mike Reynolds. He made sure he was the last to walk by, holding back as best he could. Destry kept thinking that he was the easiest to spot if lost in a crowd. He felt this kid didn't belong; maybe he happened to enlist at the wrong time and was put on this assignment by mistake. The rest of the soldiers filed by, with Mike bringing up the tail end.

Major Larson acknowledged random soldiers as they walked by, stating, "Good work, son" and "Carry on, soldier."

While the major spoke with the soldiers ahead, Destry couldn't help but look at Mike one last time. When he did, Mike formed a word with his mouth specifically for Destry and quickly looked away before the major turned back around.

"Good work, soldier," the major said and patted Mike on the back.

Mike continued to walk down the hill, nearly dragging his gun. If Destry hadn't known any better, he believed that Mike had mouthed the word "run" to him. Familiar face or not, Destry was glad to see his father-in-law, but didn't know why or what was going on. And how could he forget about the eight-foot tall whatever it was standing next to him?

With the soldiers gone, Major Larson looked at Destry and smiled. "Hang on a moment, son." He looked at the alien looming over them both and said, "I've got this." The alien continued to stare intently at the major. The major then said, "I know, but you're going to have to trust me, please."

The alien looked at Destry once more with a look of uncertainty, but didn't move and continued to watch both of them.

"So, Destry, how've you been?" the major asked.

"Ha!" Destry began. "I've been better, and I'm not sure what to even say about any of this. What's going on, Bill?"

Bill shook his head with the same smile on his face. "What are you doing, Destry? What are you doing out here?"

Destry didn't feel his explanation was even necessary compared to what Bill might be up to, but he played along. "Well, actually, I was coming from Alpine on my way back to the house. I was visiting my cousin down there, helping him out with a few things."

Bill continued to listen as he looked around cautiously from time to time, glancing back down the hill toward base. He continued nodding his head that he was taking it all in, looking back to Destry in acknowledgement. He seemed anxious. "Well, why'd you stop, son? Why here?"

"I pulled over because I was getting sleepy and didn't want to end up in a ditch somewhere. When I did, I saw something."

"You saw something?" Bill asked.

Destry looked up at the tall alien still listening to their conversation.

"Yeah, I did. So, you know, I wanted to check it out." Destry was smiling a little. Bill didn't seem so happy anymore, more nervous than anything.

"Look, Destry, I understand you might have seen something and I do understand the curiosity factor in all of this, but son, you've gotten yourself in a bit of pickle here and I'm gonna have to try to dig you out."

Destry could see that Bill wasn't playing around, and he continued to stare at Destry and back toward the base now and then. Destry wanted to leave. He wanted to get back in his truck and go to his wife. He may have witnessed a UFO and might have even been standing in the presence of an alien, but the fact of the matter was, he didn't care anymore and just wanted to go. *You're my father-in-law, what are you up to? What do you know?* He continued to look at Bill with concern. "What do I need to do, Bill? Can I leave?"

Destry heard what sounded like a hum, some sort of sound that escaped from the alien standing next to them. Both of them looked up at it.

"I know what you want me to do, but that's not an option right now. Please just give me a moment here," Bill said to the alien.

Destry looked at Bill in awe. "You're talking to it? Really? How?"

"It takes time, son, and I've, uh, been communicating with them for a while now and am able to understand."

Destry was dumbfounded, not knowing what to say. "This is amazing, but I'm feeling a little uneasy at the same time." Destry said.

"You should be, son; this isn't going to be easy."

"What exactly does this guy want you to do that you're not telling me, Bill?"

"Destry, you've seen something here that's been going on for a very long time, longer than either one of us have been around."

They both looked toward the base at the bottom of the hill while Bill spoke.

"All of this," Bill gestured with his hand. "This entire operation has been here, and probably will be, after you and I are long gone."

Destry saw for the first time what was in the other trucks: people. Civilians were being dropped off at the base. There were several people standing together, waiting for something. He could see more trucks positioned to drop off more.

"Who are those people, Bill? The ones standing in line, the ones getting off the trucks. Who are they?"

Bill sighed. "Walk with me."

He took Destry by the arm and started walking back in the direction of the freeway, into the dark. They could only go so far before losing the light that was coming from base, but far enough that the operation below the hill was not visible.

"Destry, I'm gonna tell ya because you're my daughter's husband and I'm getting old and, well, to be quite honest, I don't give a shit any more."

"What's happening, Bill?" Destry asked again. He looked back and noticed that the alien was still watching and listening, but had not moved from his original spot. Because of his dark clothes, all Destry could see clearly was that unforgettable face, which seemed to hover in the air.

"They come here every four years to Earth," Bill explained. "They show up every leap year. They come and give us information on new technologies and how to advance ourselves as a society, but only in small increments. The meeting place is not always the same, but is predetermined before their arrival."

"They do this, just because?" Destry asked.

"No, of course not. It's an exchange."

"For what, Bill? What's the price?"

Bill hesitated and looked back at his alien counterpart. "People, Destry. We exchange the information for people."

Destry's jaw dropped. He looked at the alien and back at Bill. "What do they do with the people, Bill?"

"They study them." he began, now nonchalant about the situation. "That's how they learn about us. They take DNA samples, whatever. They tell me that they're always trying to better the human race."

"And you're okay with this, Bill?"

"Don't give me that, son. Like I said, I'm getting too old for this any more. Besides, what am I really going to do about it? That's the way it is. If I'm out of the picture, another one of these cronies will take over and move up into the position. It pays the bills and I don't take my work home with me. I actually sleep well at night."

Destry couldn't get over the fact that people were being exchanged. "But who are the people, Bill? Where do they come from?"

Bill sighed. "Destry, they come from all over. Homeless people, missing people, kids and parents on milk cartons for God's sake—they're from everywhere. They're people who have been labeled as missing, unsolved murders, suicides, whatever. It doesn't matter."

"It doesn't matter?" Destry said, surprised. "Bill, you're killing people."

"They're already dead, Destry. If we don't give them people, they'll take them anyway, and maybe in a way that's not so friendly. Besides, we can't always live in the Stone Age. We're doing it for everyone—we're advancing."

"Bill, we're sacrificing people just so we can have smarter aircraft and smarter gadgets? Are you kidding me?"

"I didn't make the rules, Destry. I'm following orders too!"

The alien made the humming noise again and they both looked up at it.

"It's okay, everything's fine. Just finishing up," Bill said. "Destry, we need to finish up here and you need to leave."

"What am I supposed to do, Bill?"

"I'm asking you to do just that. I'm asking you, telling you, you need to leave now and do your very best to forget this place, forget this moment. Go home and live your life. I don't want things to get ugly here. They're trusting me to handle this because I know you. If they sense anything else, everything could change. Please." Bill held his hand out, gesturing toward the freeway.

Destry looked down at Bill's hand, then back at the alien. "I don't know about all this," he said, mostly to himself.

The alien stared back, unmoving. Destry looked at Bill and nodded, agreeing that he would leave, but Bill knew in his heart that Destry probably had no intention of keeping quiet. And someone else sensed it.

When Destry turned to walk away, he was knocked back a couple steps. The alien stood in front of him. He looked back to where the alien had been standing and thought at first it was a second one, but it was the same one. Somehow it had made its way next to Destry within an instant. Destry felt heavy and couldn't move. He could hear Bill's voice, but it was somewhere else.

"No! Not this way! Let him go!" Bill shouted.

Destry couldn't turn his head; he could only see the presence in front of him. He was drawn into the alien's eyes, looking deep within. A hand rested upon his shoulder, keeping him in place. It felt like a truck was resting on top of him. Nothing he could do allowed him to break free. Looking at the alien was like looking through a tunnel of light; nothing on either side of him was visible, just streaks of light all resonating from the center, from the alien. That's when he heard the voice.

"You have come here unwanted, uninvited. You were asked to leave without resistance, but instead you seem to forget your place, and you reject authority. Much friction is sensed within you. Therefore, you cannot be trusted. From this day forward, you will be watched. At a moment's notice, or if you become a threat to this operation, you will be removed. You have been marked."

The voice stopped and everything went black. The last thing Destry heard was Bill's voice, still shouting from someplace far away.

"Damn it! Get over here and help me . . . " Bill faded.

Destry collapsed.

12

Destry stretched in his bed, slowly licking his lips, trying to wake up. He was still hanging to the edge of a vivid dream about playing baseball. He looked at the ceiling and saw that daylight had crawled from behind the curtains and spread across the room. He closed his eyes again and drifted back to the park where he played when he was a boy. Ever since his classmate Ronny Owens had hit the ball that late afternoon in April of 1961, Destry couldn't seem to shake the nightmares of being struck over and over from the ball that damn near killed him. The doctors who treated him repeatedly told his parents that he was "one tough cookie," and just another inch probably would have "done him in."

He could hear birds singing outside his window and the continuous tick-tock from the antique Westclox alarm clock from the 1920s his mother had given him. With every second that passed, the clock took over his thoughts and pushed the birds back to their own world. His eyes grew more accustomed to the light, and his dream began to fade.

He sat up, blinking, staring off into nowhere. He tried to gather his thoughts and figure out where he was, or better yet, what had happened the night before. He glanced over to see if Cassi was in bed next to him. She wasn't. He heard noise coming from somewhere else in the house and the faint smell of coffee in the air. It was Saturday morning and she was in her normal routine of making breakfast. At least one day a week, she let him sleep until he woke on his own, usually waking up to the smell of food cooking.

He planted his feet on the floor. He took turns raising each foot, rubbing it and popping a couple of his toes. He enjoyed the feeling of the rug next to his side of the bed just for this morning ritual. Feeling the rug beneath his feet, he tried to remember the last thing that had happened the night before. He remembered leaving his cousin's house, and even remembered what they ate for dinner. How could he forget? He was still tasting some of it and his stomach wasn't too happy about it this morning, probably because of the beer.

The beer, he thought. *Why did I drink the beer?*

He knew it was going to make him sleepy and knew he needed to drive home, but he had done it anyway. Now he regretted that decision. The last time he had a hangover was months ago and vowed he didn't want to do that anymore, nor did he want to argue with Cassi about it again. He had promised not to drink if he planned to drive because he tended to black out. Once it nearly cost him after running off the road with Cassi in the truck.

I hope I didn't do anything stupid when I came in last night. I hope I played it cool and she doesn't know. What if I smell like beer? I'll say I had one, but that's it.

He figured he must have been pretty out of it if he didn't remember anything else. He didn't even recall driving, no signs along the freeway, no other thoughts or passing cars, nothing. Just popping open that first beer and then waking up.

Man, this ain't good.

He got up, dressed, brushed his teeth, and splashed cold water on his face. He ran his hands through his hair, making it look halfway decent. One last deep breath while looking at himself in the mirror. That's when there was a knock at the front door, and something didn't feel right. He continued looking in the mirror while listening. He heard Cassi open the door and begin to speak.

"Good morning, can I help you?" Whoever she was speaking to was talking too quietly for him to hear. All that was audible was Cassi's voice, pleasant but skeptical. She was acknowledging whatever was being said, but Destry could tell that she might be unsure about the situation, vulnerable.

When Destry arrived at the front door, Cassi was saying, "Oh, here's my husband now."

But the stranger had already turned away. Destry watched as the stranger walked down the porch steps toward Destry's truck, running his hand down the side of it in admiration.

"I asked him to wait. He's sure that he remembers you and said you'd remember him," Cassi said.

Destry, still watching the man, said, "What'd he want? What'd he say?"

They both looked out of the screen door, watching.

"He asked to speak to you about your truck. He wants to buy it and says he knows you'll love his offer."

Destry, surprised by the news, said, "Okay. I don't know what this is about. I didn't realize my truck was for sale. I'll go check it out. Maybe if his offer's good enough we can move to the Caribbean." Destry winked at Cassi and open the screen door.

"Be careful." She kissed him on the cheek and returned to the kitchen.

Destry walked outside, meeting the stranger at the tailgate of the truck. The man was bent over, looking at something near the license plate.

"She's a great ride and roars like a lion, but I don't recall wanting to sell her," Destry said as he stopped with his thumbs planted inside his front pockets, letting his hands hang.

As the man continued to inspect the truck, he said, "Well, between me and you . . . " the man stood and began to turn, ". . . I didn't really come to look at the truck."

They were now eye-to-eye and Destry felt like he was going to faint. Everything came rushing back to him. He felt like he was trying to take a drink from a fire hose and things weren't working out. He raised a hand to his head and took a couple steps back. He couldn't keep from staring at the man, or the young man in this case—the boy, it seemed. He grabbed hold of the side of the truck to support his weight.

"Mike?" Destry forced out. "You're real? You're the kid. The soldier."

"That's right, Destry, I'm the soldier. I take it by your reaction that you were starting to believe that last night didn't happen."

Destry shook his head from side to side in disbelief. "No. I drank a lot of beer last night and drove home. I don't remember much."

"That's bullshit and you know it, Destry. Now let's get this over with, because after today you'll never see me again, ever."

"Why are you here?" Destry asked.

"I'm here for one thing only." Mike stepped closer to Destry, his voice shaking, and glanced over his shoulder. "I'm here to make sure you understand that last night was one hundred percent real and you are officially marked."

"Marked?" Destry said.

"I didn't see it happen, but not long after we walked back to base, we saw a commotion at the top of the hill where you and the major were."

Destry strained to get every detail, trying to remember all of it and fit it back together like a puzzle in his mind. As Mike continued to speak, it was all coming together and making him feel ill. He dropped his head while listening.

"Are you all right, sir?" Mike asked, anticipating the need to catch Destry if he fainted.

"I'm fine," he said, pushing Mike's hand away. "What happened after that?"

"A few of us received the call to assist. So we returned to the top of the hill and escorted you back to your truck."

"I don't remember that," Destry said.

"Well, I should have said 'carried,' sir. We carried you to your truck and placed you in the passenger seat. You were out cold."

"Stop for a second, son. Last night when you walked away, back to base, you said something. 'Run,' I believe," Destry said.

"That's right; I did. At least that's what I felt at the time to tell you, but it wouldn't have helped. They would've caught you and things would be much different this morning."

"How different?"

"Well, for starters, you'd be dead. And possibly your family would be scheduled for pickup later in the week. What do I know? They might've taken them last night in one clean sweep," Mike explained.

Destry's mind was a whirlwind. None of this made sense, and yet it was happening. He rubbed his temples and looked toward the house to see if Cassi was listening. He prayed that she wasn't standing there. "Okay, so what next? Who drove me here? You said I was placed in the passenger seat. So how did I drive home?"

"You didn't, sir."

"I know; that's what I'm asking. Who did?"

"No one, sir. You were brought here."

Destry smiled, frustrated. "Mike, look, this is all very hard to take right now. I understand that I was in the passenger seat and brought here, that much is clear. Again, who drove the truck?"

"No one, sir, it . . . "

"Mike, someone had to drive. It didn't fly, did it?"

"Something like that, sir."

Destry stared at Mike. He wasn't sure when this conversation had taken a turn, but it just took a hard left. Destry closed his mouth and concentrated on the moment, looking at Mike for a straight answer, but afraid to ask.

"Sir. After we placed you in your truck, we were instructed to return to base. It was at that moment that I witnessed two bogies in route to your vehicle. They stopped just above your truck."

Destry was listening; his mouth had returned to the open position.

"When I turned to look back before clearing the hill, your truck was gone, sir, along with the bogies. I can't tell you what happened after that, sir."

Destry was beginning to feel nauseous again and Mike's voice was becoming distant. He slid down the side of the truck to a sitting position and drew his knees to his chest.

"It took me a while to find you. I had to ask a few of the locals if they knew you. I wanted to find you and make sure you were okay and that you knew exactly what was happening. I didn't want to think you had lost your mind," Mike explained.

"I don't feel so good, kid."

"It's gonna be okay, sir. You just can't ever talk about it, ever. They'll find you, they'll hunt you. You and your family will be in danger if you talk."

"You said I was marked. What's that?"

"They put something in you or on you. You can't reverse it or find it. It's part of you now and they can always monitor you."

"Please go. I don't wanna talk anymore," Destry said under his breath.

Mike started backing up, giving Destry some space. "I just wanted to help, sir. I just wanted to help." Mike continued to walk backward, watching to see if Destry would come back to reality. He never did.

Mike returned to his own vehicle and left. He never saw Destry again, and Destry never saw anything the same way again.

13

1992

Nash's feet began to ache. His right Achilles tendon was tender from his shoe rubbing into it. He had been so enthralled with the conversation with Kyle that it was a while before he noticed any signs of minor pains that were starting to wear on him. He had been listening to Kyle explain about the aliens—there was so much information, he felt overwhelmed. Once he felt like he had one thought settled in his mind and was willing and able to accept it, Kyle would throw something else at him. He couldn't wrap his head around the idea that the alien visitors were here every four years—and yet no one seemed to notice them.

Wow, all those people, people who will never be seen again, he thought.

Nash was actually considering the fact that Kyle was possibly lying to him just to get him on his side for some reason. He was a little worried, because if that was the case, what if Kyle was kidnapping him and making every bit of this crap up? He was definitely concerned, but leaned more toward the idea of trusting Kyle, at least for now. After all, he had protected him from Spencer, who was now in the bottom of a grave dug right in his front yard, and sharing that grave with his mother and father. Nash was not happy about that at all. He hated that his own mother was lying next to anyone who had tried to hurt him or his family. Even if his dad really hadn't been a great dad all the time, it just wasn't right.

"Kyle?"

"Yeah, kid."

"You never told me about the tooth. What was that all about?" Nash asked. "What kind of technology is that? Are you some kind of cyborg or something? Are you one of them?"

Kyle stopped and looked at Nash. "Nash, please be certain of the fact that I'm not one of them. I guarantee it. I want to help you get out of this situation."

Nash paused, thinking. He really wanted to believe Kyle, but he couldn't help remember his mother telling him about strangers and how he shouldn't trust them. He would have normally been in big trouble just for leaving the dirt road back home, but leaving with Kyle? He was too old now for a spanking. He remembered this vital piece of information clearly from the time he had broken a vase that belonged to his aunt. He never received a spanking, but did get grounded for a week.

Nash felt his eyes starting to fill with tears, and he looked away quick.

"Nash?" Kyle realized what was happening. "You missing your mom?"

Nash's head moved up and down indicating 'yes', but he continued to stare off somewhere else to avoid looking at Kyle.

Kyle stood behind Nash with both hands on his shoulders, rubbing gently. He felt terrible about Nash going through this and couldn't help but recall his own past. He knelt down, turning Nash to face him, but Nash continued to look away, avoiding eye contact.

"Nash. You know, I lost my mother also at a fairly young age. She wasn't old. She was probably close to your mother's age. She was taken from me just like you, and it hurt. It hurt bad inside me. I missed her so much, and still do."

"You did?" Nash asked, still fighting the tears.

"Yeah, kid. I did."

"And it hurt bad?" Nash asked.

"Really bad," Kyle said, smiling a little bit for reassurance. He reached up and wiped one tear away from Nash's cheek. "I promise it will be okay. She'll always be with you, little man. I can't tell you how sorry I am. Really. I am. I've done some terrible things in my life since taking on the job that I do, but I don't want it anymore. I want to get you safe. I want to try and overcome this somehow. I want to better myself, but right now, you are my priority. I have to get you to a safe place no matter what. I need to know that you believe me and trust me. I know it's going to be hard."

Nash had stopped crying and pushed his hair out of his face. "I feel a little better now. Maybe I needed a good cry," Nash said.

Kyle stood up. "I couldn't agree more. Sometimes we all need a good cry."

"I think I'm ready to keep going now. And I do believe you are trying to help me."

They continued walking. Nash wasn't really sure why he even asked Kyle about being one of them. He wasn't really scared of Kyle anymore, but was still cautious about the situation. He could still hear his mother speaking to him about strangers, but felt that Kyle was telling the truth about everything. He didn't want to take the chance of falling into the hands of someone or something not of this world, but part of him was still grounded here on planet Earth, and he was fine with that. It all seemed too far-fetched. *What have I really got to lose? It's not like I have family anymore.*

"I never really finished telling you about the tooth," Kyle said.

"Oh yeah. I screwed that up by crying like a baby," Nash said, embarrassed.

"Don't say that. It's okay. The tooth was a way that the aliens could track me. I was supposed to swallow it. Then it would have formed to my stomach lining and stayed with me forever. It was assigned to me when I joined The Corporation," Kyle explained.

"The Corporation?"

"Yeah, that's what they call our division in Washington. You know, they always have to have these fancy names for these kinds of things. Everything's always cloak-and-dagger."

Nash shrugged, but continued taking everything in.

"Anyway, I didn't swallow the chip. I was leery of the whole situation even though they told me it was standard for everyone involved. So, I had it made into a false tooth that I could get rid of at any time if I needed to."

"Better you than me. It looked like it didn't feel too good," Nash said.

"You're right about that, kid, it didn't. But, hopefully it will buy us some time."

"I hope you're right," Nash said, uncertain.

* * *

It was now silent between them and all that could be heard was the sound of their feet against the blacktop stretch of freeway. Kyle was tired of talking, and they were both thirsty. It was still hot, especially this time of year, even though it was late afternoon. Kyle had changed shirts, now wearing one of the plain white T-shirts Nash had brought. Anything was better than the long-sleeve dress shirt in this weather, especially with the bloodstain on the back. He carried his blazer and dress shirt, which were rolled into a ball with the two sleeves hanging out. He then tied those together around his waist. It reminded Nash of a fanny pack, but bulkier. Nash laughed out loud when Kyle first wrapped it around his waist and Kyle said, "Hey, Nash. Does this make my butt look big?" With that, Nash would really get going and his sides hurt from laughing.

Kyle stared out at the freeway, constantly scanning the horizon for his contact. His throat was dry, and his lips were beginning to crack in places.

He felt somewhat relieved to be able to tell Nash what had been going on. The only thing that he hadn't told him was about the ride that was on the way to pick them up.

They were just east of Crane, not too far outside the city limits. What surprised him the most was the fact that no one had offered to give them a ride. Normally, he would have had several people ask by now, but so far nothing. He figured maybe it was for the best; this way he wouldn't have to get too detailed about whom they were and why they looked the way they did.

"Kyle? I know it's probably a lot longer to go, but I'm curious about how far we'll go before taking a break."

"Well, I'll be honest with you, Nash," he said while wiping his brow. "Remember when you came out of the house earlier today, when I was standing in the garden?"

"Yeah, sure."

"Well, before you had come out, I had made a phone call to someone who could help us. They're supposed to meet us along the way and pick us up."

Nash's head shot up, "Really?" He was very excited to hear the news. "That's great, Kyle! Man, my feet hurt; I can't wait to sit down, and hopefully they'll have air conditioning in the car and we can cool off."

Kyle was pleased to hear Nash's excitement.

"Don't you worry. Trust me, there'll be A/C in the car. In fact, you can probably lay down in the back seat and take a nap if you feel like it. We'll still have a ways to go, and you might as well rest."

Nash threw both arms in the air with a loud, "Yes!"

Things became quiet again for a few minutes and they both looked ahead, watching the road.

"I just realized something, Kyle. Are you saying that you had a phone with you the whole time?"

Kyle had thought for a moment that Nash hadn't caught that. Reluctantly, he answered, "Yes."

Nash shook his head. "No, I don't want to know any more. Let's keep going. I guess you had your reasons and I'm okay with it. Let's keep going."

Kyle was surprised, but didn't respond. He didn't want to take the chance of making things worse, so he kept quiet.

"What kind of car is it, Kyle? You know, so I can help you watch for it."

"I'm not sure, but he won't miss us, I guarantee it."

"He? It's a guy?"

"Huh? Oh, I don't know. I guess it could be a girl. There are a lot of people that work for The Corporation, but I've only worked with guys so far," Kyle explained.

"Cool," Nash said, and held his head high again, watching for anyone whom might be looking for them. He stared into every car that passed by.

"I tell ya what, though," Kyle began. "If it is a girl, I'm sittin' shotgun." He gave Nash a wink and a light punch to the shoulder.

"Get outta here," Nash said, and tried to kick Kyle's backside.

Kyle only laughed at his attempt. "You're all right, kid, you're all right." Then he heard two taps from a horn.

Miguel Francisco Gutierrez La Barca III had the cruise control set on seventy-three mph. If he had learned anything in The Corporation, it was to obey all traffic laws to avoid getting the local authorities involved. He had no problem with breaking the laws; hell, that was the fun part most of the time. In this case, he wouldn't be pulled over just for a speeding ticket. It would bring up a lot of questions that he didn't want to have to deal with.

Within The Corporation, he was known as El Gato. This was the name that some of the others pinned on him due to his laid-back nature and quiet disposition. When Kyle heard about the nickname, he immediately changed the name to Felix.

Felix did like the name, and he really did like Kyle, even though Kyle was always trying to push Felix's buttons and piss him off half the time. He also earned his name because he would strike without hesitation, just like a cat. You never knew when it was going to happen.

When Felix received the call, it wasn't from Kyle, but from an unknown buried deep somewhere inside The Corporation. This was the most dangerous thing of all about The Corporation. You didn't know, and had no way of knowing, who was involved. Regardless, this wasn't anything that he was worried about. Felix was a machine; he took his calls and started moving quickly, always prepared to leave at a moment's notice.

The Ford LTD pulled out of the parking lot of the Econo Lodge no more than twenty minutes after receiving the call. All of Felix's belongings were neatly packed into a duffle bag, which he had thrown into the trunk after making coffee for the road. This job was more his style. He didn't want, and never intended, to be an agent, nor was he the office type. Staying on the move on the open road was what kept him going, and being alone for the most part was what he preferred. He had no problem with juggling his sleep hours.

He had been driving for about forty-five minutes when his phone rang again. He suspected that this might happen. Every now and then, especially on this type of run, plans would change, maybe a new location, or a change of who's getting picked up. One time his run got turned into a hit. He ended up meeting the "pick up," opened the door for him to climb in the back seat, then whacked him in the head with a hammer just as fast. He then proceeded to stuff him in the trunk and took him to another location for delivery. Felix was used to this and had no problems switching gears.

"Yeah?" he answered.

"Felix, my man! What are you doing?" Kyle said on the other end of the phone.

Felix rolled his eyes. "Why are you calling me on this line pendejo? Hello?" Felix slammed the phone back into the seat next to him after Kyle hung up, then heard his other personal phone ring. "You've got to be fucking kidding me," he said out loud.

He answered his other phone. "You're an asshole, you know that?" Felix said.

Kyle started laughing. "I love you, man! Please tell me you're on the way to pick me up. It's you, right?"

Felix squeezed the phone in his hands, only now realizing that Kyle was the person he was to pick up. This was a bittersweet relationship for Felix. "Yeah, I guess it's me."

"I knew it. There's only one agent that's Mexican enough to come out of San Angelo, Texas," Kyle laughed.

"Go fuck yourself."

"I love you too, honey," Kyle said. "Now, there's a reason I'm calling, believe it or not."

"God, I hope so," Felix said. "What do you want already?"

"How long you been driving? We're at a new location."

"Man, if you're behind me now I'm gonna kick your ass. I've been driving for about forty-five minutes and the next town is called Big Lake."

"Well, what a coincidence, I'm in a town called Big Lake, sitting inside a Dairy Queen eating an ice cream cone. So, if you get here quick enough, I might buy you one."

"You can keep the ice cream, but that sounds good. I'll see you in a few minutes."

Felix hung up.

* * *

Kyle and Nash sat in a back booth of the Dairy Queen, both eating ice cream cones. They were glad to have finally sat down for a small break. Kyle threw his dress shirt away in the bathroom trash.

The bloodstain had already set in, and he knew it was a lost cause. He was thankful that Nash had brought the T-shirt for him to wear.

Considering that Nash didn't get out of the house much, this was actually a treat for him. Kyle didn't have to ask if Nash was enjoying it. He could tell by the way he was eating the ice cream that it had been a long time since he had a reward like this. *No wonder the kid is so skinny. He's never had some good, all-American fat.* Kyle thought to himself. It was nice to see Nash in a new light, relaxed and having fun. Kyle couldn't get over the fact that this kid was sixteen. He certainly didn't seem like it.

Nash was polishing off the last bite of his cone while Kyle was leveling off the ice cream on his, just getting to the cone.

"Wow kid, you were hungry," Kyle said.

"Thanks, Kyle! Man, you don't understand. It's been forever since I had ice cream from an actual Dairy Queen. My parents brought me here one time on our way back from San Angelo. We had gone out of town for some stupid reason involving my dad, but it happened to be the day after my birthday. I think it was my eighth birthday, or fourth, or maybe my twelfth. Jeez, I really don't remember how that leap year junk works, but it really was one of my birthdays."

"It's okay, kid. I'm glad it makes you happy, and I'm glad you got to eat some. Who knows when we'll be able to do that again?" Kyle explained.

"Really? Why Kyle? You know, I never really asked, but where *are* you taking me?"

Kyle didn't want to get too detailed, but felt like he and Nash were getting closer. Since Nash really didn't have any family to speak of anymore, he certainly didn't want to blindside him, either. "I'm taking you to a safe house. Do you know what that is?"

"I think so. It's a house that's really safe? Safe from what? I think I saw a cop movie once where the main character was hiding in a safe house and no one could find him."

"Well, actually, you're right. There is a location and it's in San Angelo. It's not really a house, even though we call it that, but it's a building in a pretty nice part of town. It blends in with some of the other stores around it, so people don't pay attention."

"That sounds really cool, Kyle. Are you gonna teach me how to be like you, like an agent or something?" Nash asked.

Kyle reached out and gently touched Nash's hand, keeping him grounded. "No, no, Nash. I just mean this is a place we'll go for now so that we can form a plan about what to do next. There will be someone else there to help us make our plan and I'll introduce you to him."

Nash stared at Kyle with naive eyes. "Wow, this is so exciting, I can't wait to get there. I can't believe I won't be a secret agent, but kinda like a secret agent in training. This is amazing."

Kyle couldn't help but smile. He watched Nash, who was off in his own world, apparently still daydreaming about almost being a secret agent. Kyle popped the last chunk of cone into his mouth and enjoyed the moment.

"Kyle?"

"What's up, kid?" Kyle said.

"You've been really honest with me and I wanted to tell you something about myself. There are things you should probably know in case something happens."

Kyle wasn't sure where this was going, but he was intrigued. He was praying it wasn't going to disrupt this entire plan. *What plan?* He thought to himself, then shook the thought away. "Yeah, of course. What is it?"

"Well, ever since I can remember, my mom has taken me to the doctor off and on because of my head hurting."

Kyle nodded his head. "Are you talking about having migraines?"

"Yeah, that's it. Migraines."

"Oh man. Yeah, those hurt. I've had one before," Kyle said.

117

"Well, this is really weird. She said she took me not just because of my head but because I was saying strange things, like talking to myself. I don't remember doing it, but she said it scared her. I think it's kinda funny. I wonder what I say?"

Kyle wasn't sure whether to laugh along with Nash or not. "That is weird. Does it hurt badly with the migraine? Well, I really mean, how long does it last?" Kyle asked.

"I feel it start to hurt about right here," Nash said, pointing to the right side of his head, half way between his ear and the top of his head. "It doesn't last long, maybe twenty or thirty seconds. Then it's gone." Nash looked off and continued, "I don't really remember much after that. I just wake up and feel better."

Kyle's face was scrunched up, listening, trying to follow. "Oh, wow. Are you saying these headaches are so bad you fall asleep?"

"No, I don't fall asleep, ha!" Nash said.

"You said you woke up?"

"I guess I meant to say that I come back to whatever I was doing."

"Do you mean like a daydream, where you don't hear much going on around you and you're just in your own little world?" Kyle asked.

"Yeah, that's a good way to say it."

"Is there some sort of medicine that you're supposed to be taking? Did we forget something at the house?" Kyle was starting to get anxious.

"Well, kinda."

"Oh, no," Kyle exhaled.

"It's okay though."

"Nash, that's not okay. I'm assuming that this is something you take every day to help, right?"

"Yeah, my mom would give it to me every night before bed, but there's something that I never told her," Nash explained.

"Go on," Kyle said.

"Well, the doctors gave mom the medicine and said it would help, but I never told her that every once in a while I still get them. So, I guess it helps, but I still remember it happening a couple of times. Like I said, they don't last long, just a few seconds. The only thing that I like about the medicine is that it helps me fall asleep."

"So, it's still occurring but not as much? Sounds like the medicine definitely helped, then," Kyle said.

"Yeah, I guess so. I don't know."

Kyle had never heard of anything like this and was really trying to understand. He couldn't imagine that there was a type of migraine that lasted just a few seconds and the person lost time with no recollection. Something didn't make sense to him.

119

This story had some big holes in it, and now he really hoped this wasn't going to cause them problems.

"My mom told me about the first time I had one. She said it scared her pretty bad and they rushed me to the emergency room. She said I was sitting on my bed reading a book. It was bedtime and she was coming to tuck me in. She said I was holding my head because it had started to hurt. She ran her fingers through my hair, hoping it would make me feel better. Then she said she thought she saw a sparkle in my eye."

Kyle's face tightened, listening very carefully. "Sparkle?"

"I don't know what it means, but she said it was like a tiny star or something. Then she said it went away just as fast as she saw it, but then I said something before lying down to sleep."

Kyle looked confused. "Did she tell you what you said?"

"Yeah, ha! I thought it was funny. I must have been dreaming something pretty good. I said, 'Received' and then I think she said, 'Report' came out of my mouth."

"Received and report? What is that?" Kyle asked, still confused.

"Ha! I'm not sure, weird huh? She told me that she called my name while trying to look into my eyes, trying to get me to see her. She said I kept staring into nowhere. Then a few seconds later I said, 'Test complete' and laid down and went to sleep. She said she got my dad right then and they took me to the hospital. I guess that's when they gave her the medicine. I don't know, I don't remember that night at all."

Kyle was still bewildered, but his face relaxed and he leaned back in the booth, like something had crossed his mind.

"Pretty funny, huh?" Nash asked.

"Yeah, that's pretty strange," Kyle said, still deep in thought.

"You all right Kyle?"

Kyle's attention drifted back to Nash and he pushed his thoughts of paranoia away. "I'm good, Nash. That's a crazy story, and I don't know about you, but that ice cream was the most awesomest thing I've ever had."

"That's not a real word, is it?" Nash said.

"It is now."

"Okay, then, it was the most awesomest thing for me too."

Kyle looked passed Nash's shoulder and noticed the sedan pass by the front of the Dairy Queen. "Come on, Nash, our ride's here."

"All right! Let's go!" Nash yelled.

Many of the patrons inside stopped eating to see what the commotion was about. Kyle grasped Nash's arm. "Hey, keep it down some, we don't want to draw too much attention. Just stay calm and follow me."

Nash then spoke in a whisper. "Oh, okay, sorry Kyle."

Everyone turned their attention back to their burgers and fries, some shaking their heads at Nash for being so overzealous about whatever he was carrying on about.

* * *

Felix passed the city limit sign for Big Lake and immediately spotted the Dairy Queen on the left side of the road about another three-tenths of a mile. He slowed down as he passed it and glanced into the windows to see if he might see Kyle. He drove past, then swung wide, kicking up some dirt along the shoulder, making a U-turn and heading back. Kyle and Nash were walking outside to meet him.

Nash watched as the car got back into the right lane and headed toward them. He couldn't help but think about when Kyle and Spencer were heading toward him almost the exact same way. He wondered if he would have had time to get out of the way, had they not tried to avoid hitting the coyote or whatever it was that caused them to crash. The car looked like it was the exact same kind, black too. *Do these guys all drive the same kind of cars?*

When the car pulled up, Nash could finally see into the passenger window. He felt the hairs on his neck stand on end. Not only did they apparently drive the same cars, but the agents looked alike. This guy could have been Spencer's twin. The problem was, he was Mexican. Nash's eyes were glued on him, and he didn't want to look away in fear that Spencer part two might pull a gun out, forcing Nash to dive for cover.

Felix threw the car into park, while Nash stared at him.

Kyle opened the passenger door with a huge grin on his face. "What's up, Felix the cat?"

Felix's expression didn't change at all. "Just get in the damn car and let's go."

Nash continued to stare at Felix from underneath Kyle's arm. He slowly raised his hand. "Hi."

"Oh, I'm sorry. Felix, this is Nash. Nash, Felix," Kyle said.

Felix nodded his head and gestured to the backseat. "You've got the whole backseat to yourself if you want it, or you can sit up front with me and make this loser sit in the back," he said, and winked at Nash.

Nash looked at Kyle for approval.

"It's okay kid, Felix is cool. Just jump in the back and take a nap if you want. We've got a long ways to go."

Kyle opened the door. Nash tore his eyes away from Felix long enough to crawl into the backseat. It was more comfortable than he thought it would be. The seat seemed to form to his body and he knew he'd be asleep in no time if he let himself. Nash wasn't sure why, but he felt a little better after settling in.

Felix glanced over the seat at Nash. "Well, kid, how is it?"

"It's not so bad. I think I'll like it," Nash said, rubbing the seat on either side of him. He loved the way the cloth felt against his hands.

"Good, let's get moving, then," Felix said.

Kyle shut the door and hit Felix on the shoulder. "I love you, man."

"Bite me," Felix said, throwing the LTD into drive.

1962

It was Christmas Eve 1962. Kyle and David Hoffman were playing in the living room as early as seven-thirty in the morning, trying not to wake their parents. It had started out as normal play, but with two boys, the term "rough housing" came to mind pretty quickly.

They were up a little early for their favorite cartoons to be on yet, but early enough to raid the refrigerator and make too much noise. Little did they know their mother, Rita, was already awake, laying quietly in her bed, smiling, listening to her boys playing. She knew they could barely stand the anticipation of opening presents later in the evening. Her husband, John, was on his left side, eyes closed. He jumped when a clanging noise came from the kitchen. "Why are kids infatuated with being up so early on weekends and holidays, but not on school days?" he said.

Rita giggled. "That's what we use to do also, I'm sure. I don't know how they know, but they do," she said.

He yawned and began talking at the same time. Rita tried hard to decipher what in the world he was saying, and eventually got it. "Well, III thhink it's a dhumb rule." He cuddled up close to her, closing his eyes again. "Let's go tell them we were one day off, it's school today and Christmas Eve tomorrow," he smiled, eyes shut.

"You can try and sleep if you want, but I'm going to check on them and make some breakfast. I'm sure that's what they're looking for. David's probably trying to get Kyle to make him some bacon. You know how much he likes it." She got out of bed, threw her robe on, and slipped into her house shoes.

"Yeah, me too, that sounds wonderful right about now," he said.

"The problem is, you won't get any lying in bed."

John looked up at Rita through sleepy eyes, "Ugh. Okay, I'm coming."

"Ha, that's what I thought," she laughed.

* * *

Kyle could see his seven-year-old brother, David, hiding behind the curtains in the living room. He was wearing red-coat style, flannel pajamas, with a cowboy holster strapped around his waist. In each hand he held silver cap guns with pearl handles, but he had run out of caps back in the fall when he and Kyle had been down by the creek playing another rendition of this ongoing game of cowboys and Indians.

Kyle always had the best ideas and could come up with the best games to play, especially in the morning hours before Captain Kangaroo came on the TV. They both loved watching the Captain. David liked the Banana Man the best, but Kyle always liked Slim Goodbody. David didn't care too much for Slim because that guy really scared him. He couldn't figure out why he could see inside Slim's body. He would ask Kyle things like: *Did the guy not eat enough food? Did someone steal his skin?* After watching TV, Kyle was ready to do other things or hang out with friends closer to his age. Kyle loved his little brother very much, but he was fourteen now and at the age where he and his friends were beginning to talk about other things that a seven year old just wouldn't understand.

Kyle crouched down close to the Christmas tree, trying his best to hide behind one of the larger presents. He knew where David was hiding because his feet were exposed at the bottom of the curtains. Kyle loved the innocence of kids. They always thought they were completely hidden if their faces were covered. Kyle couldn't help but stare at David's toes that kept making little fists, pinching at the soft, plush carpet, waiting to jump out at any moment to take Kyle by surprise. He covered his mouth, trying not to laugh out loud. When he did, David must have heard something because he jumped out as if right on cue and dove into the center of the floor, firing both guns at the same time. With no caps, the guns just clicked when David squeezed the triggers as fast as he could, but he was only hitting the front of the couch with his imaginary bullets.

"Where are you?" David asked.

He looked to his right, and there was his brother charging at him, then tackling him into a ball. They rolled together on the floor with Kyle screaming, "I got you! I got you!"

"Hey! Boys, what are you doing? Kyle, get off your brother. You're going to hurt him," Rita said as she entered the room. Both boys were laughing hysterically.

"He's not hurting me, Mom. That was great!" David announced.

"Yeah, I got you good and you never knew where I was. Ha, ha!" Kyle yelled.

"Kyle, keep it down some, honey. I'm about to make some breakfast. Are you guys getting hungry?"

"Heck, yeah! I'm starving," Kyle said.

"Me too!" David shouted.

"Your dad's going to eat breakfast also, so something tells me we're going to cook lots of bacon."

Both boys froze in their position on the floor.

"Whaaat!" David said, grabbing both sides of Kyle's face, pushing his cheeks together, causing Kyle to make a weird face. "Are you kidding me?"

"Ow!" Kyle said.

David let go. "That's the best surprise ever on Christmas Eve."

"Heck yeah!" Kyle agreed.

"Well, please do me a favor and keep it down some while we cook," Rita said.

"Okay, Mom, no problem," Kyle said.

"Man, that was a good one Kyle, you did get me," David said. "Hey, is it time for the Ruff and Reddy Show?"

"I think so. We might have missed some of Captain Kangaroo."

"Ah, that's okay."

David jumped up on the couch while Kyle tuned the TV in to The Ruff and Reddy Show. There they were, and David's eyes lit up.

"Oh boy! I love it! Here we go!" he said.

Kyle placed his index finger to his own mouth, asking David to keep it down some so they didn't get into trouble. He sat down beside David, who was still wearing his holsters with the pearl-handled pistols tucked away, and put his arm around him.

* * *

It was around seven o'clock in the evening when Kyle asked his mother if he and David could walk to the Methodist Church to view the Christmas tree and lights. Every year, the church had an enormous tree that was placed in front for everyone to see. It stood at least twenty feet tall and had hundreds of lights strung throughout it. At the base of the tree was a Nativity scene, which stayed on display from about mid-December to just after New Year's Day. David and Kyle really enjoyed seeing this the most. Kyle couldn't believe the detail that went into the scene. The figures looked so real. One year Kyle thought Mother Mary was actually looking at him. However, on Christmas Eve and Christmas Day during the evening, the church had real people come and stand in, playing the parts in the scene. They even brought in real animals to make it authentic—sheep, a donkey, and even a cow were standard.

"Please, Mom, we always love to see it," Kyle said.

"I know, honey, I honestly forgot and dinner is about ready."

"Please, Mom, we won't stay long," David added. He was wearing jeans, along with a coat and a hat that covered his ears, prepared for his mother to say yes. Underneath the jacket were the holsters holding the pistols. He was at that stage where he wouldn't leave the house without them.

Rita couldn't help but smile. "Well, your father is still taking a nap. I guess we can wait a few more minutes."

David's eyes got bigger. "We can go?" he said, excited.

"I'm going to say yes, but you have to promise me you'll both be home in thirty minutes."

"All right!" David said.

"You don't have to worry, Mom," Kyle said. "I've got my watch on; we'll be on time."

Rita adjusted David's coat, buttoning his top button, and gave him a kiss on the cheek. "Okay, you two be careful and come straight back. It's been snowing a lot today and it's pretty cold."

"We will, Mom, love you," David said.

"Thanks, Mom, see you soon," Kyle said while opening the door.

The cold December air rolled in. Rita shivered and crossed her arms, rubbing her shoulders for warmth. David stepped out into the cold and planted both boots into the snow. He looked back at his mother. "Bye Mommy, I love you."

Kyle smiled at Rita and shut the door. That was the last time that Rita saw her son David, and the last time Kyle saw his mother smile.

16

The boys didn't have far to walk. The church was only two blocks away and they knew just about everyone that lived in the area. There were other families walking toward the church, as well as kids walking on their own. Nothing was out of the ordinary on this particular night. Rita and John would have been with them normally, but Rita wasn't worried. With as many people as they were friends with, she had full confidence that the two boys would be okay.

The Methodist church was built in 1910 and made of red brick. It had a dome on top with windows all the way around, which everyone came to admire. Kyle always wondered what it would be like to look out of the windows, but he was never able to find the entrance to the dome. Usually, he and David would sneak off from Sunday school and see if they could locate a staircase that might lead there. And they had heard rumors that it was a false dome, but Kyle had a hard time believing that. He would tell David, "Why build such a huge beautiful dome with windows if there was no way to have access to it?"

Kyle had always enjoyed seeing the church, as well as attending, just because of the sheer size of it. He would gawk every time he walked in. The pipe organ, which stood behind the pulpit, was huge, its pipes shooting up out the back of the organ to the ceiling. Kyle felt one of the best things to do when they were in the church was to listen to the pipe organ sing its finest tunes. There were even certain songs that were so beautiful coming through the pipes that his mother would have tears in her eyes. He remembered that one of her favorite songs was "The Old Rugged Cross." It seemed to get her every time.

As the boys got closer, they could see the top of the Christmas tree. There was a large star on top of it. It was the Star of David, lit up bright blue, and they began to hear what sounded like Christmas carols. Various people were still all around, and passersby would greet them with joyous smiles. Their community was very dedicated to the church, as well as each other. Everyone was full of Christmas spirit and would help one another with no question. When they were about three to four houses away, with the church on the right-hand side of the street, they could see several people gathering in the middle of the street and could see the glow in their faces from the Christmas lights shining down. The crowd continued out of sight, streaming up into the front of the church.

The boys came by the last house and around a huge pine tree, which stood at the property line of the church, and immediately felt the energy in the air. Their faces lit up and all the excitement that had been building up to this point was at its height.

"Oh my gosh, Kyle!" David said as he looked up to the top of the tree.

"You ain't kiddin' me. Check it out!" Kyle agreed while he pointed to the enormous star on top. "That has to be at least half the size of Dad's car, don't you think, David?"

"I don't know, but it's big! I can't believe Mommy's missing this. It's so cool! Listen to the music, Kyle."

They continued trying to make their way to the front of the crowd while looking at the tree.

"I can't see anything, Kyle. I mean I can't see the Nativity, no baby Jesus in sight."

"I can't either, not yet," Kyle said.

"Hey! Can I get on your shoulders? Maybe then I can see it and tell you how much farther."

"Yeah, okay. That's a good idea." Kyle crouched down on both knees while David climbed up on his brother. After he was in place, Kyle brought one leg out from underneath himself and planted his foot into the snow. He pushed up quick, throwing the other foot in place.

"Wow! Now I can see everything. We're almost there, Kyle."

Several people looked up at David, smiling as he passed by.

"Am I going the right way?" Kyle asked, really just to keep David busy. He was pretty sure he was cutting through the crowd in the proper places.

"Yeah, you're doing great, keep going. Hey! I can see a donkey, Kyle, a real donkey!

"Are you kidding me?" Kyle said. He was happy for David, who was having the time of his life.

Kyle began seeing the animals and some of the actors in the Nativity scene through the crowd. He finally broke through and claimed a spot right in the front. The boys looked on with wonder. There they all were: Mary, Joseph, and various animals standing about. There were sheep laying on the ground near the manger, and inside the manger was baby Jesus.

"Look, Kyle! It's not a wax doll, it's a real baby this year!" David yelled.

"Shh, keep it down David, you're yelling," Kyle said.

"Oops, I'm sorry," he said as he looked around.

A few people looked at him with smiles. They knew he was excited, and everyone was having a good time. The actors in the Nativity scene always enjoyed the little kids the most. The excitement brought from the kids boosted everyone, and the emotions in the crowd were always different. There were people crying, smiling, and sorrowful. Some sat in silence holding hands with their families or loved ones. Some were even in prayer, eyes closed, whispering to themselves.

There were Christmas carolers standing to the right of the Nativity scene singing various songs. They began singing "Silent Night."

"Kyle," David said as he tapped Kyle's shoulder. "Listen, it's 'Silent Night.' I really like this song."

Kyle slowly knelt down to let David off his shoulders. David climbed off and walked a little closer, so he could see the baby's eyes better. The actors were okay with people coming forward, and accepted David walking in. He got close and looked upon the baby. The eyes were chocolate brown.

"Beautiful," David said as he stared at him.

"Bless you, child, and Merry Christmas," the actor playing Mother Mary said to him with a wink.

"Thank you. Merry Christmas," David said.

Kyle nodded his head to her and Joseph. "Merry Christmas to you all."

Joseph stepped forward, placing a hand on Mary's shoulder, "Bless you and your families."

"Come on, David, let's let some other people take a look."

"Okay. That's amazing and so pretty, Kyle."

"I know. It really is."

They stood back for a little while and watched. They enjoyed seeing some of the other people's reactions to the Nativity scene. They both couldn't stop looking at the tree, how big it was, and the music could be heard clearly no matter where they stood. David stood in front of Kyle, leaning his back in closer against his brother. Kyle placed both hands around David, laying his hands across his chest. They stayed like this for several minutes, listening in silence. The choir finished singing their version of "We Wish You a Merry Christmas" and David shivered.

"You getting cold?" Kyle said.

"Yeah, it's really cold now. Maybe we should go. I'm ready."

"Okay, we can do that. I want to make sure you got to see everything you wanted. We probably won't get to come back tomorrow, we'll be so busy with opening gifts and visiting with family."

"Yeah, I'm okay. It was great this year. I'll never forget it. And Mother Mary spoke to me!" David said.

"That was pretty cool."

"I hope they don't keep little baby Jesus out in this weather too long. He's gonna get cold and could get sick," David said.

"I'm sure he'll be fine, David. He's well protected," Kyle reassured his brother.

The boys began walking back to their house and didn't say too much. They both could hear the carolers starting to sing, "Have Yourself a Merry Little Christmas" and David hummed along to it. There was no one on the street with them now. Kyle looked up and noticed only a few houses with their Christmas lights still on, which made the neighborhood appear darker. A light snowfall had started.

"Are you kidding me?" David yelled. "It's snowing Kyle, it's snowing!"

"I see it. I see it."

Kyle continued walking on the sidewalk while David started running back and forth from the middle of the street and up into neighbors' yards with his arms stretched out like an airplane. "This is so cool, Kyle. It's actually snowing on Christmas Eve. I wonder if Mom and Dad know."

Kyle smiled and kept his hands in his coat pockets with his shoulders hugged in nice and tight, trying to scare the chill off. It was getting colder and he was ready to get home.

"Hey, Kyle, check it out," David said.

He stood in the middle of someone's yard with both hands stretched out, face turned toward the sky, and his tongue straight out, attempting to catch any snowflake that happened his way.

"Oh yeah! Two can play that game," Kyle said.

He entered the yard and planted his feet in front of David and assumed the same position. There they both were, faces turned up, and tongues glistening in the frigid air, searching for their next meal. Their laughter was hard to control. The longer they stood there, the funnier it became. Their breaths were like small puffs of smoke, but were becoming larger clouds of vapor as they couldn't contain the giggles that followed.

The boys started to move in the yard, trying to chase the snowflakes with their tongues out in the wind. This made things even more interesting—and funny, of course.

"I got one!" David yelled.

"Whatever, I got two at the same time!"

"You lie!"

The boys continued their snowflake-eating contest until it eventually turned into a good game of tag. Tongues were tucked away, but now Kyle would slow his pace so that David could catch him and they would tumble in the snow, kicking up clouds of powder and rolling with laughter. They were facedown in the snow, trying to catch their breath when a bright light was upon them. At the same time, they heard a familiar voice.

"Boys? Kyle? David? Is that you two out there?"

Kyle looked quickly to see Ms. Clay standing at her door with a blanket wrapped around her shoulders. "Uh oh, David. We might have woken Ms. Clay up."

"Uh oh," David said.

The boys stood up as quick as they could, brushing the snow off of their clothing. Kyle took a few steps forward while adjusting his coat and hat. "I'm sorry, Ms. Clay, uh, yeah, it's me and my brother, David. We hope we didn't wake you."

Ms. Clay slowly shook her head and opened the door a little more, "No, you didn't wake me but I was just about to head that way. I thought I heard some commotion out here."

"It's okay ma'am, we're headed back to our house now. We'll see you soon. Sorry about the noise," Kyle explained quickly, and gathered up David while backing away.

Ms. Clay was a nice elderly woman, but when it came to turning kids into their parents, she didn't hesitate. Kyle learned from experience that the faster you apologized and got away from her, you were more apt to get away with it and your parents not find out. Her memory wasn't all that great these days, but if you hung around too long, she might recall all of it.

The boys walked quickly, and by the time they reached the edge of the sidewalk, they were running and laughing again.

"Wow! That was close," Kyle said.

"Yeah, it was."

As their laughter faded, they walked in silence, catching their breaths and watching the snow fall. The streets were still bare and it had grown dark. Several people had turned off their light decorations on their houses, so it was much darker from when they had left home. They weren't too far from home and Kyle could see their house in the distance, about a block away. Small bushes ran along the sidewalk in front of their house, and this time of year they were lit up bright red.

"Kyle?"

"Yeah, kid."

"My feet are starting to get cold. How much further?" David asked.

"Not much, just one more block. You probably got a little snow in one of your boots when I was kicking your ass in the snow."

David starting laughing immediately.

They would have both been grounded for sure for saying any kind of cuss words in the house, or even in public for that matter. If anyone would have heard Kyle say that, his parents were sure to find out. Kyle was very careful about what he said around David. He always made sure no one was in hearing range. Plus, he knew he could always make David laugh when he did it. David still had a large O-shaped mouth.

"Oh my gosh! I can't believe you said that. That's so funny, but you're probably right. I do think my feet are wet," David said.

Kyle laughed along with David. "Yeah, I thought you might like that."

Kyle looked up and noticed someone crouched in the middle of the street about a half block in front of them. He couldn't tell whom they were or what they were doing, but they weren't moving. *Maybe they're tying their shoe,* he thought.

"Who is that?" Kyle asked.

"Huh? Oh, I don't know. Is that one of the neighbors?"

"I'm not sure. I wonder if they need help."

As the boys got closer, they noticed that the person was dressed in black, but they were unable to see any face. He or she was looking toward the ground and wearing what appeared to be a hooded jacket, with the hood covering his or her head.

They stopped on the sidewalk. Kyle put his hand in front of David, naturally to hold him in place out of harm's way.

"Are you okay?" he asked.

There was no response from the stranger.

"Sir? Ma'am? Can we help you? Are you hurt?" he asked again.

The person made a gargling sound, slurred speech, almost inaudible.

"What was that?" David said.

"I'm not sure, but it didn't sound good. Maybe they're drunk and can't stand up."

"Ha! Maybe they're drunk off their ass!" David said, encouraging Kyle to play along.

"David, shh," Kyle said, gesturing for David to stay back.

Another gurgling sound escaped from the person.

"Pleeese helllp meh," the person said.

The boys looked at one another.

"Did you hear that, Kyle? It sounds like a man. Something's wrong, he needs help."

"Yeah, I heard that," Kyle said as he started walking toward the edge of the sidewalk. "What do you need help with? Is there someone we can call or get for you?"

"Oh yes, there is someone I need," said the man as he stood up.

He didn't look any different than the next person, just an elderly man, probably in his late seventies or early eighties. He had a smile on his face and a full set of teeth. This was probably the only thing out of the ordinary that Kyle wasn't so sure about. He guessed they were probably false teeth because they looked so good. Kyle also noticed his eyes; they were bright blue. He couldn't remember the last time he had seen eyes so bright. They were beautiful. His hair fell out from under the hood of the jacket in various places, and it was pure white.

"Okay, tell us who. Who do you need? We can get them for you," Kyle said.

He was about to step off of the sidewalk onto the street when the man raised his hand and made a small gesture with his index finger.

"That's close enough," the man said. Kyle froze.

His feet felt like lead and he was unable to lift them no matter how hard he tried. He could still bend at the waist. He could even still bend his knees. "What the hell?" he said. He reached down and started pulling at his feet. He even tried untying his shoes and pulling his feet out, but nothing worked.

"What's wrong, Kyle?" David said, walking closer to his brother.

"I'm not sure. I can't move."

David dropped to his knees and started pulling on his brother's feet, trying to help him. Small grunting noises came from deep within him as he pulled. Kyle was still bent at the knees and looked similar to a runner, crouched down, waiting for the starter pistol to be fired. He pulled at his foot just the same to no avail.

A small laugh escaped from the man's mouth as he continued to smile.

"What's funny? Do you know what happened to me? Did I step in something?" Kyle asked.

"Actually, you stepped into my world," the man said. He crouched back down, resting his hands on top of one knee.

"What?" Kyle said.

"Hello, child, remember me?" the man asked, now speaking to David. David was still pulling at Kyle's feet when he heard this, and stopped. He looked at the man like he just remembered an old friend he hadn't seen in years.

Kyle watched David. "Who is this guy, David? You know him?"

"Remember our visits?" the man said.

David stared, deep in thought, remembering an older time. He let go of Kyle's foot and stood up. "I remember you."

"Ah, that's good, you see. That's very good," the man said.

"David, what's going on? Who is this guy? Have you been spending time with this guy, without Mom and Dad knowing?" Kyle asked.

His emotions started to spin. He feared for David. He started to pull at his feet again and felt helpless. David didn't seem to notice Kyle anymore, becoming more focused on the voice in front of him.

"David. I've been thinking of you and the conversations we had. Do you remember those?" the man asked.

"Yes," David said solemnly. "Yes, I do."

"That's wonderful."

Kyle was quiet for a moment and listened very closely. He still gently tugged at his feet, but was more intent on watching what was unraveling before him.

The man continued. "That's very good, David. Do you remember my name?"

David's eyes narrowed as he dug down deep within, trying to remember the man's name.

"David, what are you doing? Who is this guy?" Kyle said with desperation in his voice. "Tell me what's going on. Let me help you!"

"Shut up, Kyle!" David said, turning and looking directly at his brother.

Kyle could see into David's eyes, but they didn't seem to be his little brother. They were from somewhere else, and those eyes scared him.

"Okay, David. Just take it easy, okay?" Kyle said.

Raspy laughter escaped from the man in the street. David turned his attention back to the man, leaving Kyle with a feeling of abandonment.

The man asked again. "Do you remember my name, child?"

David whispered under his breath, "Mr. Quick."

The man held out his hand, welcoming. "That's right, child. Please come closer. It's time."

Kyle's heart was racing out of control and his hands were sore from fighting to free his feet from their position. He stood up, almost jumping when David walked away.

"David! Where are you going? What is he talking about?"

David laughed, quietly at first, but it became louder as he got closer to Mr. Quick. Kyle teared up and couldn't begin to grasp anything that was taking place around him. The whole night was a blur.

Everything seemed fine only minutes before, and now this. His brother was not acting like his brother anymore and was about to walk off with some stranger, while he was hopelessly glued to the sidewalk and couldn't do a damn thing about it.

David finally reached Mr. Quick, paused, then placed his small arms around his neck and gave him a hug. Mr. Quick accepted it by hugging back. Kyle watched through tears and Mr. Quick stared back at him over David's shoulder, not smiling any more. Kyle saw that his expression had changed to something more sinister. He could feel his heart about to burst out of his chest. *Why isn't anyone coming out of their houses to help me?* "Help! Help!" he began to scream.

"Oh, do shut up, Kyle," Mr. Quick said and raised his hand again, swiping at the air.

Kyle became mute. He opened his mouth, screaming as loud as he could, but nothing came out. His eyes were bulging with fright. He couldn't move his feet and now he had no voice. He began to shake from crying so hard and so much. *Where are you going, David, and who is this person?*

Mr. Quick stood and placed his hands on David's shoulders. "It's been a long time, but now we will travel to meet the others. They are waiting for us."

David listened to Mr. Quick, then turned around and looked at his brother Kyle, who stared with red and puffy eyes. He felt completely helpless. He had finally given up. His arms were at his sides with no life left in them. "I have to go now, Kyle. I have to go with Mr. Quick."

Kyle stood and listened. He was drained and shook his head back and forth in disbelief. *Is he just going to turn and walk out of my life forever? Will I ever see him again?*

"You will see me someday, but that's a long time from now," David said. "I was marked a long time ago, and now I must go with Mr. Quick. He will guide me from here."

Confused, Kyle shook his head. His eyes were full of questions. He put a little pressure on his right foot, tried to lift it, but could still feel the resistance. There was no use.

"I'm sorry I yelled at you, Kyle, I didn't mean it. I will always love you, but the time is now."

Kyle started crying again for his brother. David watched but there was no sound to be heard, just his brother crying alone in silence. David's expression was solemn.

Kyle saw Mr. Quick's face began to blur and distort. The old man faded away and something disturbing started to take shape. It was a face not of this earth, nor of this planet; it was alien, and the eyes grew brighter in color, more electric looking.

Mr. Quick raised his hand and Kyle's feet finally let loose from the ground. He stumbled to the ground, letting out a cry of pain from cracking his knees on the pavement, then fell forward, landing on his forearms. He pushed himself up and looked at his brother. "David!" he yelled, staggering to his feet.

Kyle ran. Mr. Quick placed his hands on David's shoulders and they both disappeared into a vapor. Kyle watched in shock as it lifted into the air and was swallowed up by something dark. He couldn't see any stars in the sky. Something blocked them. Within seconds, a dark object began to move and lifted faster into the sky. It was gone in a flash, leaving only a thin trail of clouds chasing after it.

Kyle dropped to his knees in the middle of the street and screamed for his life. He screamed for David. Porch lights in the neighborhood began to light up, and people began coming out of their homes to see what was going on.

John and Rita Hoffman sat in the waiting room of the Lafayette Psychiatric Hospital. Kyle had been making regular visits now ever since David disappeared nearly seven months ago.

The night David went missing, Kyle was found by several neighbors, who in turn contacted his parents to nearly drag him out of the street. He was in a frantic state, and remained that way until the police arrived. It was then that he started to calm down enough to try and explain what had happened.

For three days, Kyle sat at home, barred up in his room, and barely ate anything. During that time, the only thing his parents could get down him was water and occasionally soup.

His parents were a mess too. They began to fight at first, but by the time the police returned to the house with more questions on the third day, they had begun to communicate again, hoping the police might have had some sort of lead in finding their son. It was also on this day that Kyle was hospitalized for psychiatric evaluation and underwent heavy questioning from the police in the disappearance of his brother. The lead investigator on the case was a Detective Mullins. His report, filed on Friday, December 28, 1962, stated:

In all my years serving on the police force, and working with the missing persons division, I have never encountered an individual with a more unbelievable story, that is, surprisingly enough, believable.

Mr. Kyle Hoffman has in no way, shape, or form strayed from his original testimony, and all facts remain constant and accurate within the timeline presented to the Indiana State Police from the morning of the date in question until time of occurrence.

Lafayette State Police

Lafayette, IN.

Incident Report #80071103

Report Entered: 12/28/1962 20:19:05

Reporting Det:

Mullins, William (467)

Rita dozed to the sound of John slowly paging through a magazine in the waiting room. Her head lay softly against his shoulder. She was thankful that Kyle was no longer required to be at the hospital under surveillance, on lockdown as they say. She knew that Kyle was not responsible for what had happen to David; she felt it. But, just as frustrating as it was for Kyle to have to tell the same story over and over without anyone seeming to believe him, she was exhausted from feeling like she had to explain herself to everyone around her. Not to John, of course, they were both on the same page and trusted their son. Really, what did it matter what other people thought? It didn't. They did the best they could with what they had and no one could change that. Someone else might have an opinion on what they could have done differently, but that didn't necessarily make it right for her and John.

She tried to place herself in a nonbiased position and really listen to Kyle, and not only try to understand what he might have experienced, but put herself in that position also. *Were the things he said true? Was it really possible?* She found herself questioning Kyle's childhood and if there might have been anything that he would have had resentment toward, anything that would have made him act negatively toward his brother. This was the police getting in her head again. She tried to push it further out, away from what she truly believed, but maybe not too far.

* * *

Kyle left the small room at the end of his last evaluation, and headed back to the waiting room to meet with his parents. *What a shithole, this place*, he thought. Every last inch of him ached with sorrow for David. He missed his brother so much, but in the past seven months he felt he'd been poked, questioned, accused, and even coerced into acting a certain way. The last thing he was able to do was mourn. Today was the last day that he had to see the psychiatrist, appointed by the state, and he had been cleared as a suspect for at least a month now. He choked up when he shut the door behind him and walked down the hall, but was unclear where the emotions were coming from. He assumed it was from every direction. He had been through so much, and finding David was all that mattered now.

Kyle walked across the lobby into the small waiting room on the other side of the reception's desk. It was deathly quiet; not a sound could be heard from his tennis shoes sinking into the light blue plush carpet. He looked at his mom and dad sitting close to one another and knew in that instant what love was all about. His parents were always there for him and his brother, and even though David was missing, they never gave up hope, especially now. Through this whole mess, both of them had been by his side every step of the way—every doctor's visit, police statements, and interviews, they were there.

Kyle placed one hand on his dad's knee. "Hey, Dad."

John looked up, surprised, "Hey, son. Well, how'd it go? Good?"

"Yeah, everything went smooth, looks like I'm all done," he said.

Rita sat up, catching the end of it. "Oh good, so you're all finished? It's official?"

Kyle flashed a few papers that he held in his hands. "Yep, all official. I got every seal of approval right here."

"I'm so happy for you. I know it's been a long time," she said. She stood up and gave him a hug only a mother could give. They both felt it. She cried.

John held his hand out to Kyle. "You did good, son. I'm proud of you."

"Thanks, Dad," he said as he shook his dad's hand with confidence. "I think I'm ready to get out of here and put this place behind me."

"I don't blame you one bit. Are you hungry?"

"Starving."

"Me too," Rita said.

They gathered up their belongings and walked to the door.

"Hey wait," Kyle said. "I'm gonna stop in the restroom first before we hit the road. I'll meet you in the car."

"Yeah, okay," Rita said.

Kyle entered the restroom. It was the same color as the carpet in the lobby. *What's with all the light blue?* he wondered. The restroom was lined in blue tile, and a single urinal hung on the wall next to two stalls. It was empty and he was glad. All the interactions he'd been having the past few months had been overwhelming at times, and he was ready to try to start putting things to rest and concentrate on remembering David.

While he washed his hands, he heard the door open, followed by footsteps. They stopped at the sink next to him. He hated when other people were in a public restroom with him. It weirded him out a little, everyone standing so close at times. He enjoyed his privacy more than this.

"Well, you're finally going home, huh?" the man asked.

Kyle didn't expect to be carrying on a conversation in the restroom with someone he didn't know. He was nervous and started to back away from the sink, maybe even run.

"It's okay, kid. I'm not some pervert and I'm not going to hurt you. I just want to ask you a question."

"What?"

"You're Kyle Hoffman, right? You're the one that saw the little green men, they say."

"Is that what they say?"

"Come on, kid, it's been all over the news the past few months. I know who you are."

"If you know who I am, then why'd you ask?"

"Touché, kid. Touché." The man threw is paper towel in the trash and offered his hand to Kyle. "My name's Spencer."

Kyle was hesitant at first, but stepped forward and shook his hand. "Hello Spencer, I'm officially Kyle Hoffman."

Spencer smiled. "You're all right, kid. Listen, I know your parents are waiting so I'll make this quick." He crossed his arms and leaned against the sink, crossing his feet. His sunglasses were pushed back on his head. "I work for an organization, a secret organization."

Kyle smirked and started to back away again.

"Now, wait a minute, kid. Before you get that look on your face, hear me out."

"All right, no problem, but please hurry."

"I work for an organization that interacts directly with the subjects *you* say you encountered seven months ago."

Kyle stood staring at Spencer. He was stumped. David was the only thing going through his mind right now. "Wait a minute, what?" he asked.

"I think you heard me just fine, kid. Now, listen up. You're way too young now, but if you're interested, I would like to offer you a job."

"Are you serious? This stuff is real? I mean, I know it's real, but are you saying that you believe me?" Kyle had started to sweat and now stood closer to Spencer.

"Yeah, that's what I'm saying. I believe you. *We* believe you." Spencer stood up and took a business card from his breast pocket. "Here ya go. That phone number you might want to memorize. Then I'd burn it; don't leave it lying around."

"If this place is so secret, why are you telling me?" Kyle asked.

"Because I believe in you, kid, and I know you want answers. I believe you'll have a chance at finding those answers, too."

Kyle took the card, glanced at the number, and put it in the front pocket of his jeans.

"Don't forget, you're not old enough yet. So go home and live your life. Be with your parents and remember the good times with your brother. You two were close. Get some closure." Spencer lowered the glasses back down over his eyes and turned toward the door. He grabbed the handle, still facing the door, "When you turn eighteen, and if you're still searching for answers, call. We could use you."

Kyle watched as Spencer left. He went to the sink and splashed cold water on his face a couple times. He looked at himself in the mirror, staring deeply within his own eyes. "I know you're out there. I don't know where, but I'll find you. I promise, I'll find you. Then I'll bring you home."

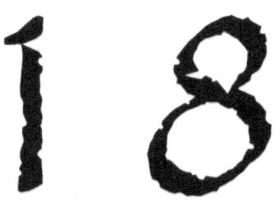

1992

Nash rode in the back of the LTD, his head swaying from side to side. He couldn't seem to keep track of time. He had no idea how long he'd been riding now; it felt like hours. His head was leaned back against the seat and rolled to and fro. His eyelids were heavy and would shut, taking him in and out of sleep. His thoughts bordered on dreams and reality. His mind seemed to be racing; thoughts of his mother skated in and out, and sadness would enter. He missed her so much. Then his thoughts went to his father. His feelings didn't seem as strong. He wasn't sure why he wasn't sad like he was about his mother. He didn't miss him as much, but at the same time he felt sorry for him. He wanted to hug him one more time, like he used to when he was younger. Nash slept.

Nash walked down the street happy and content with life, and overall, just being a kid. There were several shops to see and hundreds of people out doing the same, looking in store windows, and carrying bags of swag that they had just purchased. He saw kids in all directions with their parents having a good time, eating sugar-filled treats such as chocolate and hard candies, which seemed you could buy at every fourth or fifth store in a row. This place was designed scientifically to draw people in and keep them there, to keep shoveling money into the money-making machine.

He walked along the strip saying hello to various people. Some folks seemed concerned because he appeared to be alone; he was. Nash didn't notice why this was odd to them and continued having a good time. He was looking for something or someone, but wasn't sure which. He felt lost and found all at the same time and was in a particularly good mood. The smile on his face was inviting, and it was magnetic to be around him in this moment.

He came across the next candy shop and decided to slip in and take a peek. A large sign hung above the entrance that read, "Sweetness." He couldn't believe the size of the place when he walked in, and the amount of candy on display was insane. It was immediate brain overload. The color spectrum table in his head red-lined off the chart. There wasn't a color not represented, and some seemed to be brand new. He saw candies on a large display inside the door: Butterfingers, Red Vines, Baby Ruth, and M&M's. Beyond that, running all along the center aisle were various hard candies such as Skittles, Nerds, Gobstoppers, Harry Potter Bertie Botts Beans, Life Savers, and something new to him, Toxic Taste. All of these candies were in acrylic bins with large metal scoops available so that anyone could get as much as they wanted—by the pound if need be. He couldn't imagine anyone wanting to buy that much candy, but he figured there might be people in the world who liked to stockpile this stuff at home and eat a little at a time. His favorite was chocolate. There was something about the hard candies, especially the sour ones, that drove him crazy. He couldn't eat them, or in this case, he couldn't even look at them without salivating profusely. He looked around the store, stretching his mouth open, trying to make it stop.

"Can I help you find something?" he heard someone ask. He turned and saw a girl about his age, probably in high school, staring at him. She wore a red-and-white striped dress with a small, white apron tied around her waist. The dress was short, cutting off right above the knee and he was really enjoying it. She had blonde hair pulled up under her visor hat, with the rest of it pouring out the top and falling back into a ponytail. Last, a small, black name tag that read "Sam" stared at him from the top of her left breast.

Nash looked up slowly and connected with her eyes. "Um, hi," he said.

She let out a quirky laugh and shifted her weight. "Are you looking for something in particular?'

"I can't believe how much candy is in this store. I've never seen anything like it."

"It's amazing, right? I haven't been working here long, but it's so much fun. I still don't think I've tried everything in here, but it's a goal," she said.

Nash continued to stare at her with uncertainty; something was making him feel uncomfortable and good at the same time. Something was moving in his pants. "Wow, I wish I could work in a place like this. It's amazing."

"Cool! If you're really interested, I could get you an app to fill out. Like I said, it's really fun."

"It's okay, I don't want to fill one out today, I just want to buy some chocolate."

"Okay. What kind of chocolate are you looking for?" Sam said.

"Do you have any chocolate-covered almonds? Those are my faves."

"Oh yeah, we definitely have those. Follow me." Sam walked toward the back of the store. Most of the chocolates were located along the back wall. Nash followed. He was finally able to get a good view of the whole place, but the only thing he seemed to be taking in was the hip displacement in front of him. He was mesmerized by the back and forth movement until she stopped abruptly, and he almost plowed into her.

"I'm sorry," Nash said.

Sam laughed nervously. "It's okay. All right, here are all the chocolate-covered everything you can think of. You said almonds?"

"Yeah, almonds, those are the ones my mom buys for me."

Sam smiled and looked away quickly, grabbing a large scoop and digging deep into the almonds. "How much do you want, a pound?"

"Uh, I don't know if . . . "

"If you get a pound it works out cheaper," she said.

Nash was getting nervous; he was slow with the numbers. "Sure, give me a pound, thanks."

Sam finished scooping the large helping of almonds into the bag, twisted it up into a knot and tied it off. Nash's face lit up as he stared at the bag. "Wow, my mouth is starting to water already and so is my jaw," he said with a grin.

Sam looked at him, disturbed. "You have a nice day." She turned and walked away, looking back once. Nash couldn't figure out what he said that was so strange to the girl. He thought she was nice and hoped to talk to her again sometime, but something told him she was done.

He walked to the counter, set the bag of chocolates down, and laid a five-dollar bill beside it.

"Did you find everything okay today, sir?" the man behind the counter asked.

"Um, yeah, it was fine. These are my faves," Nash said, pointing at the bag.

The man smiled back and began punching keys on the register. "That'll be $5.35 please."

Nash stared at the man. He grinned from ear to ear, only thinking about sinking the chocolate into his face. The man looked back at Nash and gestured toward the money on the counter. Nash finally looked down, picked up the five and held it out for the man to take. "Here ya go, buddy."

"Ah son, that's not enough money. It's $5.35."

Nash's grin started to droop, and he fell even further in embarrassment.

"What do you mean $5.35? It said $4.95 on the display for a pound. The girl, Sam, she assured me it was a better deal," he said as he pointed her out in the middle of the room.

Sam heard her name and glanced quickly toward the register. The man behind the counter held up his hand for Sam to stay where she was, letting her know everything was okay. He scooped up the five dollars, threw it into the drawer, and closed it tight. "I tell ya what, kid, don't worry about the thirty-five cents, maybe next time you can make it up. It's just a simple mistake."

"Oh wow! Thanks mister. I really appreciate it. These are my faves and I can't live without my faves." Nash picked up the bag and started untying the small bow at the top.

The man watched Nash walk out of the store, stuffing chocolates in his mouth. "See ya later, kid. Thanks for stopping by Sweetness."

Nash held up his hand, "No prowbem." At least that's how it sounded. His mouth was already full.

He walked on the sidewalk and continued to shovel in the candy. He thought that this was absolutely the best day ever. People glanced at him as he walked by and he would grin a chocolaty grin at them. This is the one thing that he felt he could eat and not get tired of. However, he had already polished off about half the bag and seemed to be slowing down. Now he was thirsty. He realized he hadn't planned for that, and remembered that he gave the last bit of money he had to the guy at Sweetness.

He looked around frantically. He was standing in front of what looked like some sort of flower and plant store. It said, "Floral Design Boutique" on the sign. He certainly didn't need any flowers, but figured they might have a water fountain in there somewhere or maybe even a bathroom where he could get a drink from the sink. He walked in.

When he closed the door behind him, it was quiet, real quiet. The fragrance in the air was exhilarating, and he loved it. He loved the smell of fresh flowers. They reminded him of his mother. From time to time, she was able to get some for the house, but that didn't happen often. When she did, though, Nash was just as happy. They seemed to brighten up the whole day.

"Hello?" he said.

It seemed like nobody was there. Everything was beautiful and well kept, but no one in sight. Finally, he heard something, some sort of movement coming toward him.

"May I help you?"

Nash looked up to see an older woman, probably in her seventies, walking slowly toward him. She looked as if she had a hard time walking, so he walked toward her a little bit to shorten the distance. "Uh, hello ma'am. My name is Nash. Do you happen to have a water fountain?"

"A water fountain? No, I don't, but you look pretty desperate for water. Are you okay?"

"Uh, yes ma'am. I'm fine. I just bought these." He held up the bag of candy for her to see and grinned as widely as he could.

The woman smirked. "Well, I can imagine after eating a few of those you probably are thirsty. My name's Vera. Let's see what we can come up with. Follow me."

She walked toward the back of the shop and Nash followed. They rounded a section of wall that separated the main showroom from the back. Nash noticed that this part of the store was where they made their displays and did all the prep work for the flowers. In one corner of the room various tools were scattered about. He even saw portable electric saws and a drill, probably for larger displays. There was a large aluminum trashcan with sporadic wood shavings scattered on the floor.

He continued to follow Vera, who headed to the opposite side of the room to a kitchen area. There were several cabinets running along the ceiling and above a refrigerator. There was even a small microwave in one corner of the countertop, which ran along the wall. Just opposite the countertop and refrigerator was an island consisting of a large stainless steel table. Connected to the table, also stainless steel, was a large sink where things could be washed or watered.

"Now, let's see. Honey, you're taller than me, open that first cabinet there and look inside. You'll find a coffee mug or cup that some of the employees use. One of those should be good for a drink of water."

Nash realized how small this woman was. He thought he was short at five foot five, but she only came to his shoulder. He looked away quickly when she caught him sizing her up and pointed. "Um, this one here?"

"Yes, that's the one."

Nash opened the first cabinet and saw several drinking options to choose from. Some glassware, but mostly plastic. Almost all of the cups were from some type of festival or annual event that happened in town. Some were even from out of town, maybe bought during a vacation and brought here to live out the rest of its life because the owner of the cup had too many at home similar to it.

"There ought to be something there. Just grab what you like."

Nash studied a couple of them. One was a large thirty-two-ounce cup from Sea World and had a large picture of Shamu on the side. He chose a white coffee mug that had four simple generic black letters written across it: S.S.D.D. He smiled when he saw it because he knew exactly what it meant. Same shit, different day—it always made him laugh. He reached for the mug and turned around. "I'll take this one," he said, looking at Vera.

She twisted the edge of her mouth up, questioning the cup. "Okay, well, here ya go." She gestured to the sink. "Take all the water you need."

Nash filled the cup once and downed the water. Without hesitating, he filled it again, and then a third time. He was halfway through the third cup when he finally slowed enough to catch his breath. He set the cup down on the edge of the sink and exhaled. "Wow, I was thirsty. I guess I ate more of the chocolates than I thought. I can't help it sometimes."

"I'm glad you got your fill. If you're done, I'll walk you back to the front of the store."

"Yeah, sure. I'm ready."

On their way out of the back room, he noticed several long-stemmed roses that had been placed into a long box. "Wow, those are beautiful," he said, stopping to gawk.

Vera turned to see. He was staring at the gift box that she had been working on when he first walked into the store. She walked back to the table and stopped beside him, looking down at the flowers as they lay in the box. "What do you see, Nash?" she asked, watching for his reaction.

Nash stared deeply at the roses. "I see love. I see peace. Mostly, I feel this moment right now, an overwhelming feeling that everything that's important is now. Nothing else matters."

Vera nodded, lips closed tightly.

Nash knew that there were a lot of people in the world that concentrated and believed in the moment of "now" more than anything. They didn't seem to worry about the future and had learned to let go of the past. He felt that it came to him naturally to feel this way about life, but wasn't sure why. He never seemed to worry about much. He just lived in the moment.

Vera took time to look at the roses also. It brought a smile to her face, standing there with him. "Would you like to hold one, Nash?"

"Really? Can I? I would love to!" He watched as Vera carefully removed one of the roses from its resting spot in the gift box. She laid part of the tissue paper to one side so she could place it back in its exact position when she returned it.

"All right, here you go. Now isn't that beautiful?" she said.

He held onto the stem and bent the rose toward his nose. The anticipation was killing him. When it reached him, he drew in a long, deep breath, sending his senses into orbit from the fragrance. It made him laugh out loud when he smelled it. "That's great! I love it!"

"It is a gorgeous smell." Vera watched, still smiling.

"That's the most beautiful thing ever, thank you."

"Absolutely, Nash. I could tell you needed that."

"I'll be taking this with me," he said.

Vera looked at him inquisitively, not clear what he meant. "Well, I guess you could, but maybe a different one. This one is already sold and has its place back in the box," she said patting the top of the gift box.

"Oh! No, I'm sorry. I don't mean I'm actually going to keep it. I mean I'll take it with me in my heart. I'll never forget it." He held the rose out to her. "You can have it back now."

Vera reached for the rose. "Oh okay, I understand. Well isn't that nice, Nash, that you're able to keep it for yourself and always remember. Maybe you can come back again sometime and actually get one, you know, to keep. That way you could see it every day and smell it, too."

"If I took one home, it would only fade in time and that would make me sad. This way I can remember it like it was."

Vera paused. She respected what he had to say. When she took the rose from him, a single thorn caught the inside of his thumb and dug in good.

Nash winced.

Felix passed the city limits of San Angelo and slowed the LTD down to the local speed. They had been driving a little over an hour and Kyle's head rested back against the seat, facing the passenger window. He slept quietly, with his hands folded in his lap. Nash was curled up in a fetal position in the backseat and seemed to be sleeping just as soundly. A small bit of drool had escaped the corner of his mouth and soaked into the plush fabric of the seat. They were both exhausted from their morning escapades, but it was hard to say who was more tired than the other: Kyle, fighting for his life with Spencer, or Nash, who had just lost both parents. He was mentally drained not just from that, but from everything Kyle had told him about the uninvited guests who show up every so often to take our own kind for their advancement. Even though they were making it seem like we were getting a great deal, we weren't. The people of Earth were the ones getting screwed in the end. They were never going to let us advance too quickly, and we would never catch up to them. We would always be kept in a position of want or need, and eager for more.

Felix pulled up in front of the safe house and parked the car. They were on a busy stretch of road in the middle of town, which happened to be right in the middle of a strip mall. There were all different kinds of stores linked together. Talbots, J. Crew, Nike, and Banana Republic lined the side of the street where Felix parked.

Several people milled about, in and out of different stores. It was just another Saturday as people spent their hard-earned money on the very things they loved so much. No one paid attention to Nash, Kyle, and Felix. They were just another car on the street, a few more bodies to add to the equation of a typical weekend. Everyone else was doing what they do best—spending money.

Felix sat in silence watching people as they strolled past. Kyle opened his eyes and saw a wide variety of flowers displayed in storefront windows. He lowered his sunglasses from the bridge of his nose to get a better look. The colors jumped out at him. He squinted, letting the light soak into his tired eyes. Only the sound of the engine still running could be heard from inside the car; no one spoke.

While Felix and Kyle stared out of the passenger side window at the flower shop, Nash shot straight up and took in a large gasp of air, his face almost touching the glass in the backseat. Felix and Kyle jumped at the sound.

Nash loved to sleep, not because he was lazy, but because he loved to dream. Dreaming meant he was able to go on a different adventure every night, sometimes funny or just plain weird. He had never had a nightmare before, and he wasn't sure why, but deep down he wasn't so sure he really wanted to experience that. Whether it was people trying to kill you, monsters gnawing your arms off, zombies crawling through your window, or someone grabbing your foot when you dangle it off the bed while falling asleep, he was convinced that having a nightmare didn't sound fun at all.

"Nash? You okay?" Kyle asked.

Nash continued staring out the window, still in a daze from waking up. He had beads of sweat gathered on his forehead and his lips were glistening from drool. "Where are we?"

"We're in San Angelo. We're here, at the safe house. You must've had a bad dream or something. Don't worry, we're fine."

"Yeah, must have," Nash said. He could see various people walking past the car along the sidewalk, shopping bags in their hands, some with children following. He had a sense of deja vu but couldn't remember his dream at all. He could see flowers in the store window across from him, and it gave him a sense of happiness and dread at the same time. His eyes turned upward, above the door to see where they were, and that's when the hair on his neck stood straight up. Written in a beautiful script, Floral Design Boutique stared back at him. "What kind of place is this? Do we need flowers for someone? Did someone else die?"

"Floral Design Boutique." Kyle said.

"I see that, but why are we here, Kyle?"

"This is it, kid. This is the place we've been driving to, the place to regroup and get you safe."

"Kyle? I really like flowers. I think they're really pretty and all, and my mother really liked 'em, but I really don't think I want any right now. How much farther do we go to get to the secret hideout with the other guys like you and Felix?" Nash looked at Felix, who gave him a small, quick wink, then he turned his attention back to the flower shop.

Kyle laughed a little. "Don't worry, kid, we're not buying flowers today. You'll just have to trust me on this one."

"It'll make more sense when you get in there, Nash," Felix said.

Nash continued looking out the window.

"Well, I guess this is it. Felix, I can't tell you enough how much I appreciate the ride out here." Kyle held out his hand and Felix accepted it.

"No problem. You want me to wait around to make sure everything goes okay?"

"Nah, we're good, man. I'll call if I need you. Nash? You ready?"

"Yeah, sure."

"Take care of him, Kyle," Felix said.

"I will."

Kyle stepped out of the car and shut the door. He opened Nash's door, letting the fresh air roll in, which helped ease Nash's nerves. "Well, you comin'?" Kyle asked.

Nash looked up at Kyle.

"Take it easy, kid," Felix said.

Nash turned and nodded at Felix, "You too." He got out of the car and Kyle closed it behind him. They both stepped onto the sidewalk and began cutting through the crowd. Nash couldn't help but notice certain things about different people, still feeling a little dizzy from his dream. *Why can't I remember?*

Kyle was already through the cluster of people and almost to the door of the shop, but Nash was still tangled up in his thoughts, as well as a few strangers. "I'm sorry, excuse me," he said as he bumped into people, trying to look around at the same time, taking in everything that he could.

"Pardon me. I'm so sorry." This even escaped his lips after running into a woman, making her purse slip off her shoulder. She looked at him, irritated.

"Be careful," she said.

He turned, ducked his head, and ran directly into someone else.

"Ouch! You stepped on my foot!" he heard a girl say.

When he was able to back away from her, the first thing he saw was the name tag. It read "Sam." It was pinned onto a red-and-white-stripped dress. He made eye contact with her and started to sweat.

"That really hurt. You should watch where you're going."

"I'm really sorry, it was an accident."

It was then that he realized this was the girl from the dream he had in the car. The candy girl. "Hey, you work in the candy store . . . uh . . . Sweetness, right?"

"Ha, ya think?" she said, gesturing to her outfit. "What gave you that idea? You should be a detective.

Please move, I'm late." She pushed past him and continued walking, now with a small limp and an attitude.

Nash stood for a moment, watching her walk away. "She was so much nicer in the dream. I wonder what happened? I hope it wasn't me," he said out loud.

"Nash," Kyle called, beckoning him with his hand to follow. He stood at the entrance, holding the door open, letting Nash take the lead.

Nash entered the store and the fresh scent of flowers captivated him. He was back in his dream. He wanted to tell Kyle about the dream, but hesitated. Something told him to keep it to himself for now.

*** *** ***

It was beautiful inside. The colors alone were almost overwhelming. Everywhere he turned was gorgeous; not a dull moment existed here. "It's so quiet in here, Kyle," Nash whispered.

"It's okay, Nash, you can talk normally. There's not anyone in here except for a few of our employees that handle this side of the safe house. You'll meet whoever is here today."

"You mean this really is a safe house? But what about all these flowers? I don't understand; this looks like a store, not a secret agent hideout."

"Look, Nash, this is what's called a storefront. To all the people walking by, it seems like a normal flower shop. People can come in, shop, look around, whatever. They don't know any differently. However, in the back of the store, there's another part that only a few of us know about."

"You mean the people with The Corporation?" Nash said.

"Exactly. That's how we operate throughout the world. You never know where we are, if you're a, well, a normal person, that is."

"So, I do get to see a secret agent hideout after all, huh Kyle?"

"Yes you do, my man." Kyle placed his hand on Nash's shoulder. "Let's go. Just follow me."

They walked through the store and into the back room. Again, Nash was taken back to his dream. He spotted several supplies in a corner, various tools, and he noticed the kitchen. It was the same. There were the stainless steel sink and the refrigerator.

"Well, well, I wondered if you were working in here today," Kyle said.

Nash turned to see who Kyle was speaking to and felt chills shoot through him.

"Oh my goodness! Well if it isn't Kyle Hoffman." She walked past the table where she had been working and gave him a hug.

Nash was still in shock that he was seeing someone else from his dream and kept wondering if something was wrong with him. This had never happened before.

"You look great! I can't remember when I saw you last—five, maybe six months?"

"Yeah, probably something like that," Kyle said.

Nash watched as they spoke, still confused about the whole situation and not feeling so well. He felt hot and needed to sit down.

"Well, it's wonderful to see you. So, who's your helper these days?" she asked, looking at Nash.

"This is Nash. Nash, this is Vera."

Vera held out her hand and smiled. Nash stared, dumbfounded from the name "Vera" still knocking on his brain. She looked at Kyle with concern.

"Nash? You okay? This is Vera," Kyle said.

"Oh, I'm sorry," Nash said finally, and held his hand out.

Vera reached a little farther, grasped it, and shook with authority. "Well, it's very nice to meet you, Nash. I hope that you and Kyle work out well together. Let me know if you need anything at all."

"Actually, I could use some water. I'm kinda hot."

"I was about to say you look a little pasty. You feel okay?" Kyle asked.

"I think I'm just nervous," Nash said.

"Well, no need to be nervous around me, darling. I can dance with the best of 'em," Vera said, walking toward the kitchen. She poured Nash a small cup of water and brought it back. "Here ya go, honey, maybe this will help."

"Thank you." Nash took a drink from the coffee mug and Kyle began to chuckle. "What's so funny, Kyle?"

"I remember that cup. I've drank out of it before. It always made me laugh, but Spencer didn't care for it."

Nash turned the mug around to the other side, and saw the letters: S.S.D.D.

"I don't know if you know this or not kid, but that means 'Same Shit, Different Day'." Kyle laughed out loud and Vera smiled. Nash couldn't take it anymore and began to sway. The cup started to drop.

"Whoa! Nash!" Kyle yelled, grabbing the cup and handing it to Vera. "What's wrong?"

"I think I just need to sit down. It's been a long day."

Vera started feeling uncomfortable. "Maybe you should take him on back and let him rest a bit."

"Yeah, I think you're right. Come on, Nash, it's okay."

They walked side by side, and Nash turned his head, looking back at Vera, "It was nice to meet you, ma'am."

"Oh, nice to meet you too, Nash. You take care. Get some rest."

Nash nodded and let Kyle guide him to a security sealed door located at the back of the room. Kyle punched a series of numbers into the keypad, letting them through.

20

When they stepped through the doorway, Nash expected to see all sorts of high tech computers and instruments. He hoped to see technology that he had never heard of, possibly things that were not even invented yet, at least as far as the public was concerned. To his surprise, it almost looked like the back room to a library or storage facility. He saw a dark hallway opening up into a small room with a desk and computer. All along the hallway leading up to the room were several boxes with large amounts of paperwork filling them. Some were messy and some were very organized with bright color-coded tabs to mark certain items of importance. At the end of the hallway, opposite the desk, was a couch. It was a very old couch with a few holes, and some of the holes were large enough that the mustard-yellow foam interior poked out.

He couldn't see anyone in the room, but beyond the small room was a larger one. Maybe the person they were meeting was in there.

"All right, here we go, Nash, ease back this way and we'll get you comfortable."

"I feel really dizzy," Nash said.

"Yeah, no kidding. You looked like you were gonna drop right on the floor in front of Vera." Kyle walked Nash to the couch, and they plopped down into place, both letting out heavy sighs and sinking into the worn-out couch.

"Ah, that's nice," Kyle said. Nash agreed.

"Who's there?" Eddie Black said as he rounded the corner, swinging a gun from side to side. He and Kyle had become friends while they were recruits for The Corporation. However, Eddie had been battling ADD and Tourette's all his life. Therefore, becoming a full-fledged agent wasn't written in the stars for Eddie.

"It's okay, Eddie, it's me, Kyle. There's no need for the gun. By the way, what are doing with a gun? I thought you weren't supposed to have one."

"Yeah, well. That's what they get. They took my gun and gave me a bat instead, a fuckin' bat! What am I supposed to do with a baseball bat you must be asking yourself, right?"

"I'm not sure Eddie, what *do* you do with a baseball bat?"

"I hit the fuckers in the arm and said, 'Now give me my gun back.' That's what happens when you give me a bat."

"Nice work, Eddie."

"Fuckin' A! Not takin' my gun! You know why?"

"Still got me, Eddie, not really sure."

"Because it's mine!"

"That's what I figured," Kyle said, smiling.

Nash was amused watching Eddie rant. He wasn't sure what to think about him, but was enjoying the show. Kyle looked at Nash, and Nash's eyes were questioning who this guy was. Kyle made a circular motion around his temple with his index finger, suggesting that Eddie was "loo-loo."

Eddie wandered off a few steps, searching for something in the piles of boxes t in the hallway. Then, without warning, he returned, off on another rampage. "Ok, what? So, now you're here, which I didn't know you were coming here. Fuck! And not only are you here, you've brought a guest with you. Well, isn't that nice? A guest. For me? No, you shouldn't have. Or wait a minute, is the guest for your entertainment? Oh no! I got it. He's for both of our enjoyment, right? He's like a jester and he's here to make us both laugh, because this is already so goddamn funny!"

"Eddie," Kyle said.

Silence filled the room. Eddie's face suddenly transformed into an inquisitive angel with tight lips and wide eyes, mocking Kyle. He started nodded frantically, already agreeing with anything that Kyle had to say.

"We've both been through a lot, you and I, and I seriously hope that you can hear me out and trust that I'm here for a damn good reason. I know it's without warning and I deeply apologize. I know that you don't care for surprises at all of any kind and I respect that. And again, I apologize for our intrusion on your privacy. This is Nash, and he has suffered a terrible loss, losing both parents, due to me and Spencer."

Eddie looked frantically back and forth between Kyle and Nash with the same condescending look.

"So, if you have a moment, please let me catch you up to speed. Please accept our apology."

Eddie's head was still moving up and down, almost quivering. His eyes darted back and forth. "Fuck!" He stormed off, ranting.

"Well, that went well," Kyle said.

Nash felt unsure. "He seems like he's still upset."

"Oh no. He's good now. He accepted our apology, didn't you hear?"

Nash wasn't sure what to say, and Kyle was already lifting him by the arm, helping him up to join Eddie in the next room.

They left the hallway and stepped into a larger room. Nash wasn't really sure what he was seeing but there were all sorts of different electronics, most of which he had only read about in comics and never thought he would actually see first-hand. He figured he was finally seeing what he had expected when they first walked in. He saw at least seven different computer monitors, all displaying something different. "Whoa," he said to himself.

Eddie heard this and spoke up immediately. "Hey, don't make a big thing out of it, kid. It's just a little technology."

"A little? This place is crazy. What all do you do here?"

Eddie's face showed all the typical signs of worry, but Kyle was there to help out. "It's all right, Nash. I don't think Eddie's up to explaining everything in the room right now."

"Yeah, there's a lot that goes on here, kid, so try not to knock anything over. Just don't touch, or at least ask." Eddie shook his head and walked away, mumbling to himself. Kyle reassured Nash it was okay and to be careful.

Eddie stopped. "Hey kid! There's a video game system back here if you're in to that kinda stuff."

Nash's eyes brightened and he looked at Kyle for approval.

"You like video games, Nash?"

"Uh, I'm never played one, Kyle. I'm not sure."

"Oh wow! I think you'll like it a lot. Go on back with Eddie and he'll get you fixed up. Go on, it's okay. I'm gonna stay here and wait for Eddie. We need to talk about some things."

"You guys are going to talk about me, aren't you?" Nash asked.

"There's no foolin' you, Nash. You're right, we are. But, that's not a bad thing. I need to see if Eddie can help us get things in order and get you safe, okay?"

Nash's eyes wandered away, looking toward Eddie, who was cussing about something. He looked like he was tangled up in a big mess of wires of some sort. Nash laughed and looked at Kyle. "Yeah okay. I better go help Eddie before he hurts himself."

Nash walked to Eddie and tried to help him detangle the mess of wires that were hooked to the game system and controllers. Nash didn't know what was supposed to plug into what or how the thing worked, but did his best to watch Eddie and go with the flow.

"Okay, kid, there are only three games I have that are really worth playing. You can look through them all if you like. It's these three here." Eddie pointed to the stack of games on the coffee table next to the game system.

Nash read the titles. "Super Mario Bros., Kung-Fu Master, and Duck Hunt."

"That's right, and like I said, the others are over there in the box next to the TV."

"Okay, thanks Eddie. I think I'll be fine."

* * *

Kyle sat quietly at a large desk rolling a pencil back and forth between his fingers. It wasn't actually a desk, but a large, six-foot table with Eddie's computer system and assortment of monitors all snaked together. He watched as Nash and Eddie worked together and wondered what to do next. His mind kept drifting back to his brother, and all he could do was wonder how to save Nash from that same fate. Ever since that night with David, he wondered if he would see Mr. Quick again. After all this time with The Corporation, he had never heard anyone mention the name. He guessed it was just a name that was made up at the time. Maybe that person still does exist, but he goes by something else. *Hell, they're aliens,* he thought. For all he knew, none of them had actual names. Kyle felt he could go crazy trying to figure it all out.

"Well, that ought to keep him busy for a while. You want one of these?" Eddie held out a beer in a long-necked bottle to Kyle. He already had his bottle turned upside down against his lips while holding the other one out for Kyle to take. When Eddie set the bottle down on the desk, Kyle noticed that half of it was already gone.

"Thanks Eddie. I probably need this right about now. My head's just a whirlwind."

He heard Eddie take a deep breath and let out an exhale that didn't seem as if it were ever going to end. Eddie sat down, propped his feet on the desk, and held the beer bottle in his lap. Kyle couldn't help notice that it made Eddie look like he was holding his own manhood out for the whole world to see. He smiled. One thing was for sure, he had known Eddie long enough to understand that alcohol was the only thing that seemed to calm him down. Afterward, he was able to carry on a normal conversation with just about anyone without getting worked up. Kyle was glad about this, especially knowing what he had to explain next.

"Well I have to admit, Kyle, it was really great to see you when you came through that door. It's been a long time. I was surprised to see the kid with you. I never pegged you as the type to bring your work home with you, but hey, all's good. He seems like a good one, maybe a little slow. What's his story?"

Kyle took a drink from his beer then rolled his lips together, savoring the taste.

"That's good beer," he paused. "The story with Nash," he began, looking toward Nash, watching him play the video games. It looked like he was enjoying himself. He was even talking out loud and dodging something, moving from side to side.

"Whoa! No, not that way!" Nash yelled.

Kyle smirked. "That kid's been through a lot, Eddie."

"I'm listening," Eddie said, taking another drink from his beer.

21

Kyle finished getting Eddie up to speed. Eddie now had three empty beer bottles beside him and a little less than half to go on the fourth. Kyle had stopped at two.

"So, once we got in the car with Felix, I knew where we needed to go. Here. I knew you would probably have the best advice and if not that, at least understand what I had to do."

Eddie sat forward with his elbows resting on his knees and mouth open, listening to Kyle. It wasn't a look of surprise, but a look of exhaustion from a long-winded conversation. Kyle could tell by the look on Eddie's face that he was shocked at the situation.

Eddie took the last swig from the beer bottle and set it on the desk with the others. "Kyle? What have you done, man? Seriously? They're gonna find you. There's only so many places you can go. Besides, there's so many people walking around this godforsaken place that work for them. You never know who or where they are."

"You?" Kyle said.

"No, not me, others. It could be anybody walking up and down the street out there. You never know."

Kyle noticed that Nash was looking in their direction, trying to hear what they were saying. "Kyle? You guys okay?"

"We're fine, Nash, just talking. It's . . . okay."

"That kid's in danger, Kyle, and so are you," Eddie said.

Kyle sat forward, moving closer to Eddie, almost knee-to-knee. "I'm not worried about me right now, Eddie, but I am worried about Nash. I want to get him to a safe place. I want to keep him here, let him have a life of his own and not go with them. You know they'll experiment on him and possibly kill him after that."

"Are you considering making a deal with them? A trade? They're gonna take you anyway and now maybe me if you don't get outta here."

"I understand that, Eddie, but I don't think you're hearing me. I need your help! Do you get that? Please help me. You owe me, dammit!" Kyle said.

Kyle had just dropped an anchor in Eddie's lap.

Eddie's lips tightened. "So, that's it, huh?" He sat back in the chair, a light scoff escaping his mouth. "You know, people throw that type of language around all the time, 'I owe you one' or 'I've got your back,' but I guess I didn't think you'd play that card right now, not with this. This isn't just your life on the line, it's all of us—including my mother."

Eddie's face had grown red and he stood, pacing back and forth in the small space, shaking his head. "Jesus Christ, Kyle! I mean, seriously, what the fuck?" He ran his hands through his hair and even pulled a little, his frustration showing through very clear to Kyle, who did feel bad for putting Eddie in this situation. But he also knew deep down that if anyone was to think of something spectacular, it was Eddie.

"Holy shit!" Nash exclaimed as he dodged left and jerked his hands right with the controller.

"Nash! Keep it down over there."

"Sorry, Kyle. I guess I got a little excited. It's so realistic. You really need to try it."

"Maybe later, kid, now's not a good time."

"Yeah, okay," Nash said, continuing to play the game. He was already ducking and weaving again almost in perfect time to the continuous, melodramatic, monotone music that was piercing into Kyle's skull.

"How do you stand it?" Kyle asked, rubbing his temples.

"Stand what?" Eddie said nervously, oblivious to what was going on.

"Never mind."

Eddie stopped and looked as if he had just realized the most amazing thing in the world. He had one hand on top of his head, the other reaching out in front of him, grasping at the air.

"Eddie?"

"Shh, shh, wait!" he said, swinging his arm in Kyle's direction, just in case the thought was about to escape and he didn't want to let it get away.

"You gotta be kidding me. You gotta be fucking kidding me," Eddie said while walking into the next room. He went down the hall and toward the door leading into the flower shop.

Kyle watched as Eddie disappeared. This was the moment he was waiting for. The moment Eddie had "the spark" is what Kyle liked to call it. He smiled to himself, knowing Eddie was on to something. He just hoped it was good enough.

"Ma!" Eddie yelled. "Ma! You there?"

"Yes, I'm here. Why on Earth are you screaming, Edward? There could've been someone in the shop."

Kyle listened to the conversation between Eddie and Vera. He had heard these types of conversations before and they all seemed to end the same. Vera would put Eddie in his place, and Eddie would have the most magnificent revelation of plans along with having to apologize to his mother. Kyle couldn't hear them anymore; they were too far away. He stayed put at the desk and watched Nash play the video game. He was surprised how well Nash picked up on the games. He looked like he was having fun.

Kyle heard the door open, signaling that Eddie was coming back from the flower shop. Along with a large clatter, Eddie yelled out, "Ow! Piece of shit folding chair!" This was followed by a few more moments of things being readjusted in the small hallway and several more colorful metaphors escaping from Eddie's mouth. Kyle could tell that the alcohol might have started to wear off a little from the way Eddie was acting.

Eddie walked into the room with a confident look on his face, holding something in his hand and desperately looking for something else.

"Eddie?"

"Hang on a sec, Kyle, almost ready."

He continued toward the back of the room where there were more large file cabinets and an additional room. Kyle heard several key lock codes being punched into another keypad and the sound of locks releasing. He had been in that room with Eddie before, and remembered it being a small room, but large enough to contain a couple of upright medical-grade laboratory refrigerators. They were the kind with the solid glass doors on the front, housing different types of medicines or vaccines. In Eddie's case, his contained more experiments and unofficial drugs used by The Corporation. There were also two different types of stainless steel sterilizing instrument trays and a large supply of syringes. Eddie had full clearance from The Corporation and was able to do any type of experiments deemed necessary for the benefit of the company. Almost all of his studies were conducted on animals provided to him, but during the years, a human would fall through the cracks when official business became a priority.

Kyle saw the light turn off and the sound of the door locking behind Eddie, along with the keypad chirping out a single audible tone, indicating that it had been reset back into a locked status.

"All right, Kyle, here we go." Eddie said as he approached the desk. In one hand he was holding what appeared to be a small vial and a syringe still in its packaging; in the other, two more beers.

"You keeping booze in the medical supply room these days?"

"Up yours, buddy, it's my room and besides, the coolers work better than this piece of crap out here." Eddie kicked at the small General Electric fridge. Its fan was making a low rubbing sound every now and then, but stopped when Eddie planted his foot on it. He set himself down in front of Kyle while looking to see if Nash was still playing video games. He was acting cautiously and spoke quietly, urging Kyle to move in closer.

"Holy shit!" Nash yelled out with excitement.

"Nash!"

"Sorry, Kyle! This is so cool."

Kyle turned back to Eddie, who was looking at him with several beads of sweat on his forehead and a crazed look in his eyes. "All right. You're going to have to trust me on this one, but I think I've got this figured out."

"You've got my attention. What is it?"

"Long story short, there's this certain Corporation agent, formerly a soldier, who now works a desk job but still maintains a certain privileged security clearance."

Kyle rubbed his forehead. He had heard this before and knew that it was going to entail something that could get them in deeper than they already were. *We're already too deep as it is. What would this matter?* he thought to himself.

He brought himself back to the conversation and Eddie's voice came back into focus.

". . . Anyway, he was sort of an outcast, I believe, but was here one time speaking with my mother. He gives us information from time to time if he feels it will benefit us, and keeps us up to date on some of the other drugs being used, especially if I'm not cleared to get them. Well, this just happens to be one of them." Eddie held the vial up between his index finger and thumb, presenting it.

"Do I know this person? You said he's one of ours," Kyle asked.

"I don't know if you would or not; he was never an agent. I probably shouldn't tell you that crap, though."

"That's true, I probably don't want to know who he is, but tell me what this stuff is and what it's supposed to do."

Eddie placed the small 10 ml vial into Kyle's palm. He studied the label, trying to find the name of whatever it was, but found nothing other than generic warnings indicating that it was a sample and for animal treatment only. Along with this information was what appeared to be a lot number and an expiration date, a month later. The vial itself was clear glass, and the liquid inside was bright yellow. It reminded Kyle of urine after someone had taken a lot of vitamins.

"So, this stuff should help you get to where you're going without being followed," Eddie said.

"How's that possible? Does it make us invisible or something?"

"No! But, yes! You won't be able to be seen. I'm not talking about Claude Rains here, I'm talking about not being able to be tracked."

Kyle became more interested and looked deeper at the liquid rolling around inside the vial while Eddie explained.

"This serum came to be after several of our own were getting tagged by the ETs. Supposedly the ETs had some people of concern that they wanted to watch, you know, keep an eye on and see what they were up to, if they were trustworthy. Well, The Corporation figured it out after those who were being watched turned up missing. These were high-level officials—the ETs were taking them! They always seemed one step ahead and were seriously messing things up for our boys. Anyway, we figured out what they were doing and one of our brainiacs came up with this." He pointed at the vial in Kyle's hand.

Kyle raised up the vial, swirling the liquid around in the light, watching it. He looked at Eddie. "Go on."

"You give the host a small dose of this stuff and it completely wipes out the tracking capabilities of the device that was originally planted."

Kyle's lips separated and his eyebrows raised. He looked over at Nash playing his games and back at Eddie. "Are you serious? This could really work. This could be the break I was really looking for."

"Well, let's not get too carried away. I mean, they are ETs. Who knows really what other means they use to find people. But at least you could get a head start."

Kyle lowered his head, a little discouraged.

"Hey, I'm not saying it won't work. Maybe he could get lucky and they stop looking. What do I know? But it's a shot, right?"

"You're right, Eddie, it's a shot. The problem is, we don't know if it will work." Kyle pointed at the label with his thumb, holding the vial for Eddie to see. "This says here, animal testing only."

"Yeah well, a bottle of aspirin says take two for adults, but don't tell me you haven't taken four after a hard night drinking. Am I right?"

"You have me there, but I don't want him growing a zebra's tail either."

"But if he grew a third leg, he'd be thankful right?" Eddie smiled.

Kyle gave Eddie that disapproving, motherly look that this was not the time for jokes.

"Okay, okay, I know it hasn't been tested on humans, but I do know that it is completely safe. No harm has come to any of the animals, only minor hiccups," Eddie trailed off.

Kyle's eyebrows spiked. "What kind of hiccups?"

Eddie stood up and stretched, feeling the need to walk. "The only thing I know about is some possible memory loss. What's it really matter? You told me that he had been through a lot, that he lost his parents. What could be better than some memory loss? That's the perfect prescription in a time like this, huh?" Eddie rubbed his chin, showing his intellect. "We could all probably use some memory loss."

Kyle's head dropped, looking down at the floor. He could hear the video game still spewing out various sounds and the continuous, hypnotic music. Nash was lost in the moment and enjoying himself. Kyle felt happiness for him and wanted it to continue. The real question was, could he trust Eddie enough to try this drug on Nash? Or really not Eddie, but the person who brought it to Eddie and Vera in the first place. If he did it, and it worked, Nash may have the best chance yet for a fresh start. It was really the ETs Kyle was worried about. They'd probably continue looking for him, and he was pretty much screwed when it came to keeping his job. He couldn't run forever. He knew in the end he'd probably have to go with them or take his own life, and he wasn't too keen on that idea. At least if he went with them, he might get to see David again. He figured he was doing all of this for David.

"I don't know what else to do, Eddie, but I feel like I can trust you. I just don't want to see Nash hurt."

Eddie sat down and took the vial, then placed a hand on Kyle's shoulder. "He'll be all right; this stuff works. Besides, if there's no tracker in him, it does nothing, that's all it does. Well, then there's the zebra tail thing."

Kyle shook his head. "You're sorry, man."

"There's that smile. Now let's do this," Eddie said. He stood up and started preparing things.

Kyle stood too and said, "I can't do it."

"What?"

"I mean, I can't stick him."

"You gotta be kidding me. Now I have to do that, too?" Eddie said.

"Please Eddie."

"All right, fine, I'll do it. Why don't you go get us some coffee or something. Tell my mom I love her so she won't gripe too much about me ranting earlier."

Kyle agreed. "Yeah that sounds good, I'll do that. I'll come back in about fifteen minutes or so. Is that enough time?"

"Uh, yeah, that should work."

Kyle turned to walk away then stopped himself. "Eddie?"

"Yeah?"

"Please explain to him as much as possible before doing it. Let him know it's essential and why. Remember, he's been through a lot."

Eddie's face tightened. "I got this. Just call it thirty minutes then. Take your time and I'll get him playing games again."

"Sounds good, see you soon." Kyle walked down the hall and entered back into the flower shop, leaving Eddie and Nash alone.

Eddie walked over to where Nash was playing and stood behind him. "Hey, Nash, can I talk to you for a sec?"

Nash paused his game and turned around. He looked at Eddie, then past him, scanning the room. "Where's Kyle?"

"Uh, he had to step out for a moment. He went to get us something to drink. Don't worry, he's coming back."

"Yeah sure, I can talk, but I'd like to finish my game."

"This won't take long, I promise. Come on over here to my desk."

Nash set the controller down and followed Eddie.

22

Kyle took a long, deep breath after entering the flower shop. He realized that after being in the back for that long, he really needed some fresh air. The air seemed to be stale where Eddie was; he couldn't imagine being cooped up in there most of the day every day. But, he knew that was more of what Eddie was all about. He was able to do such tasks and had the patience of Job. He could outlast anyone when it came to staying in one place in excess of what was needed.

Kyle was going to check on Vera, maybe see if she wanted some coffee also. He needed some neutral conversation, if that was even possible right now. He heard voices, then noticed Vera had a customer in the store. It had to be her last customer, judging by the time. It had been a long day, and it was getting late. Kyle felt his body for the first time really starting to give. He wished he could lay his head down for a few minutes, but knew that wasn't going to happen right now. There was too much to do. One thing he did notice was the fact that he was still wearing the same clothes from the morning and he looked pretty bad.

He found the restroom, located next to the small kitchen area, and cleaned himself up. He took his shirt off and used the soap from the dispenser to clean up under his arms, chest, and hands. Then he washed his face, and pushed the cool water back through his hair, slicking it back. *That was better than nothing, in fact that was fabulous,* he thought.

After washing up, he returned to the kitchen to make a cup of coffee. Vera was standing close by, throwing away a few items, trying to get the store ready for closing. He noticed she had already turned off a few lights and the front half of the store was dark, with the sign in the window reading "Closed."

"Oh, you startled me," Vera said.

"Sorry about that, I was cleaning up a bit."

"Oh, I don't blame you. It was hot out there today. Where's Nash? Eddie?"

"They're still in the back going over some things. I needed to take a break and make a cup of coffee."

"You left Nash alone with Eddie? That's scary." She laughed. "Let's hope he doesn't wear off on him too much. Eddie's definitely a handful."

Kyle agreed. "Yeah, he is, but a good man."

"True. He's got a lot of heart."

"Yes, he does."

Vera ended up making the coffee, and they sat at the stainless steel countertop together. "So, what's to become of Nash, Kyle? What's your plan? Eddie came out earlier raving on about something we obtained quite a while back."

"I don't want to say too much, but he's in danger. I want to help him, keep him safe."

"That's nice, but who's going to save the rest of us?" she said.

Kyle looked at Vera and realized what she meant. It was as if someone had just turned all the lights on in the room. Vera was referring to everyone, humans.

"Eventually they'll get him, Kyle, even if you save him now. Whether it's his children, if he has any, grandchildren and so forth. In the end, they always win. I sometimes wonder if we ever really had a chance way back when. What if we would've said no the first time they came around?"

Kyle sipped his coffee and listened. This was the first time he understood the gravity of the situation. She was right, and there wasn't anything he could do, no one could. "I never really thought about it that way before until now. They really are everywhere, aren't they? Always watching us, I mean."

"I believe so. No wonder the government doesn't say anything. Can you imagine the paranoia, what it would do to people?"

"But there are so many that want to know. Why can't we make our own choice?" Kyle said.

"I don't know if that would be possible. There are too many people in this world that think we are nothing but the result of evolution, a speck of dust that just happened. Besides, who's going to tell them, you?"

"Ha, not me! But wouldn't it be amazing if they did know for once? To wake up and realize that we're not alone. Maybe once they knew that, we as a people could learn and advance ourselves on our own, without the manipulation from them. Who knows, maybe they would stop taking our own and work with us instead of against us." Kyle drifted off, rubbing the top of his thumb with his index finger, picking at the dead skin.

Vera watched Kyle from behind her coffee mug, taking another sip, not sure if he was with her or not. He seemed distant, delusional.

He looked up, almost making Vera jump. "But who am I kidding, right? They're not going to believe just one guy. I'm not sure what's going to happen to me anyway."

"What's that supposed to mean?" Vera asked.

Kyle took another drink of coffee. "I don't want to give up on Nash. Once I get him safe, once I feel like he's safe, I'll probably have to turn myself in to The Corporation. I really don't have anywhere else to go. I'm thankful that you and Eddie have allowed me to be here without saying anything. I know it's a risk."

"You are always welcome here, Kyle. You know that."

"Thanks, Vera."

Kyle finished off what was left in his mug and stood up, stretching. "Well, I guess I should go back in and check on them. You need anything out here, any help?"

"No, I'm good. I'm going to rest for a few minutes, then leave."

"Well, it was good to see you again," he said, leaning over to give her a hug.

"You too. Don't be a stranger."

* * *

When Kyle closed the door behind him, the first thing he noticed was the quiet. It struck him in a way that didn't seem right. He walked in the next room and found Eddie and Nash sitting at the desk staring at one another. They weren't moving.

"Hey, how's it going?" Kyle asked.

Nash looked up at Kyle. "Oh, it's going." Then Nash looked back at Eddie, who was staring at Nash with a look of horror and confusion. "Edward here wanted to give me a shot."

Kyle sensed a different tone from Nash that he had never heard before. It seemed more aware, more mature. "Oh yeah? It wasn't that bad, was it?" Kyle asked.

Nash looked at Kyle again. "I guess not. It did hurt though, a little." He looked back at Eddie. "It wasn't very nice."

Eddie still said nothing and finally looked at Kyle. There was a different look about Eddie. He seemed quiet, concerned, maybe scared if Kyle was reading him right.

"Nash, why don't you play a few more games," Kyle said.

Nash was still looking at Eddie. Then he stood up and went into the next room.

Kyle watched as Eddie started putting things away, cleaning some items off the desk. "Eddie? Is everything all right?"

Eddie gave an indifferent shrug. "Yeah, we're good."

Kyle wasn't sure what to think of Eddie's new attitude or why this was happening. *Did they get into an argument or something?* "Eddie, I'm not sure what's going on, but something seems different. Are you really okay? Did Nash say something that upset you?"

When Eddie finished throwing some items away, he turned and leaned against the desk. "Yeah, I'm fine, and no, nothing happened. But we do need to talk."

"I'm listening."

"Now that this is done," he paused. "Now that this is done, I think it's time for you two to leave. I think it's time to take Nash somewhere else."

Kyle couldn't help but wonder what in the world had changed in the past thirty minutes or so that was causing Eddie to talk this way. He's always been direct in his own way, but not like this; this was different. Kyle didn't want to push the issue because he was unsure where this was coming from. This seemed like a different Eddie. "I'm not really sure where to go, but I'm sure we can figure that out. It's getting late, but maybe a motel is our best bet right now. I certainly don't want to put you out any more than we have."

Eddie nodded his head, agreeing with Kyle. "Yeah, I think it's time. I'm sorry Kyle, it's my mother.

I'm thinking of her and this situation. The more I think of it, well, it's under my skin and I don't . . . I want her safety as well as my own right now."

Kyle understood Eddie's concern and his mind relaxed a little after hearing his explanation. He couldn't blame Eddie for thinking this way and probably would have felt the same had the tables been turned. He agreed with him and Eddie could see it. "All right, no problem. Just give me a few minutes to speak with Nash and we'll try and get out of here soon."

Eddie nodded.

Kyle went to Nash and told him that it was time for them to go. Eddie watched, but could hear nothing. He watched as Nash set down his controller, as Nash looked at Kyle with concern, and as Nash's eyes found him again, staring back over Kyle's shoulder, still sour about the shot. Eddie looked away and made himself look busy. He heard some noise and looked back to see that they were putting the games away and packing things up.

"Kyle?" Nash said.

"Yeah, Nash."

"Where are we going now? What's the plan?"

"Well, because of the shot that you took, we can pretty much go where we want.

Nash stopped putting things away. "Shot?"

"Yeah, the shot. The one you just got." He continued packing things away, "I think the best decision now is to make our way to a motel and get some food, maybe some rest. What do you say, you hungry?"

Nash still felt confused. "Food does sound pretty good right now. What about Eddie?"

Kyle made sure Eddie wasn't close by, "Well, Eddie and his mom live and work here in town. They're staying. Don't worry, they should be fine, but it's not good for us to stay here."

"Because of *them*, right?" Nash said.

"Yeah, that's right. I like to call them ETs or Greys."

"Greys? Why do you call them that?" Nash asked.

"That's easy. Because that's what color they are, or at least they look that color. C'mon, it's best we go. We don't want to put them in any more danger than we already have," Kyle explained.

They finished gathering the few personal items they had and found Eddie in the back room checking his medical supplies, looking for something. His head was buried deep inside one of the medical refrigerators.

"Eddie?" Kyle said.

Eddie pulled his head from the cold and looked at both of them with that same distant look, still bent over behind the glass door. He wore reading glasses on the crook of his nose, trying to read various labels on vials. Nash raised his arm, bending at the elbow only, giving a single wave, but said nothing.

"Hey," Eddie said, then raised the glasses, pushing them back onto his hairline.

"We've got our stuff and are getting ready to leave. We put the games back where they were, so things should be in order," Kyle said.

"Okay, sounds good." Eddie set a vial back into the refrigerator and stood up, closing the door. "So, that's everything I guess? You're all good?" he asked.

"Yeah, we're good."

The tension in the room was extraordinary, but Kyle tried to keep moving or talking about anything to avoid it. He could see that Eddie was ready for them to go and didn't have anything else to say.

"Well, we don't want to take up any more of your time than we have to. We should go now." Kyle offered his hand.

Eddie stepped forward and took his hand with a firm grip and looked him in the eyes. Kyle felt he could see sorrow in Eddie, but stopped himself from saying anything. He guessed that Eddie felt too bad and didn't know how to express himself. He had put up with them the past few hours, putting himself and his mother in harm's way. Now he was asking them to leave. *How else was he supposed to act?* Kyle thought. He couldn't blame him. He leaned in quick and gave Eddie a one-armed hug. "You hang in there. It was good to see you."

"You too, take care of yourself." Eddie said. He looked down and noticed that Nash held his hand out, offering to shake.

"I'm sorry," Nash said.

Eddie slowly took Nash's hand and began to shake. "It's okay. I think we're good now. You?"

"Yeah, I'm good. It was nice to meet you," Nash said. He turned and walked away, going toward the hallway leading back to the flower shop.

Kyle watched. "Well, that was odd. I guess he's ready to hit the trail."

"Yeah, I guess so. Well, again, take care of yourself," Eddie said.

Kyle nodded and clapped Eddie on the shoulder. "See ya. We'll let ourselves out the front door, just don't forget to lock it up behind."

Eddie watched as Kyle and Nash walked back into the flower shop and closed the door. When the door sealed shut behind them, he started crying.

23

Kyle was already on the phone trying to figure out the best place to stay for the night after leaving the flower shop. He was also watching for someone that he might ask, someone local.

"Hey Kyle, there's a 7-11. Why don't we grab something to eat?"

"Sure, kid, that sounds good," he said while fumbling with his cell phone.

Nash's senses were heightened as soon as he opened the door to the 7-11. He could smell hot dogs, pizza, and just the sight of the soda fountain made his mouth water. He then spotted the candy aisle, which made him think of Sam from the candy shop. There was every single kind of chocolate that he could ever want. He was damn near drooling.

"Kyle! Come on, this is great," he said.

Kyle was hanging up his phone to another dead end and trying to watch Nash at the same time. "Yeah, I'm coming, hang on." When he got inside the door, he could smell the food as well, and it was good. He stood for a minute or two with his nose turned up toward the ceiling, like a dog finding a scent. Their last meal had been the ice cream cone and that didn't hold them for long. Then the ride with Felix and hanging out with Eddie all evening. They were starving.

"Kyle, look!"

He walked over to see what Nash was looking at and found him with his nose pressed tightly up against the glass of the hot dog warming machine. His eyes were round and mouth hanging open, staring. The hot dogs slowly turned in their synchronized, steam-filled box, with the aroma seeping out of the top.

"You guys need help?"

Kyle looked up quickly to see a small-framed girl standing to his right, behind the counter. She looked to be all of five foot three, but probably about ninety-five pounds soaking wet. She was very thin and pretty. She was young, probably nineteen, with jet black hair cut with bangs. She didn't wear a lot of makeup; she was naturally pretty, with blue eyes.

"Uh, we're looking at the hot dogs. I mean, we're going to get some food, but not sure what yet," Kyle explained.

"I think *he* wants a dog," she said, gesturing with her head toward Nash.

"Yeah, I think you're right. Nash, you want one?"

"Can I? Yes, I want one, maybe two."

The girl raised her eyebrows and laughed. You can have as many as you want darlin'. Nash's face finally pulled away from the glass, and he looked back at the girl, then to Kyle. "I'm gonna get two dogs, and she called me darlin'." Nash said. He thought he was whispering but the girl caught most of it.

"Wonderful," Kyle said. He looked at the girl's name tag and it read "Basha." "How do you pronounce your name?"

"With a short 'a' sound," she said, sounding it out for him. "Bah-shah."

"Oh cool, that's nice. I like that."

She smiled back at him. "What else you gonna get? Pizza?"

Nash's eyes lit up again.

"No, Nash, you're not getting pizza, too, but I am. Yeah, give me two slices of pepperoni, please," Kyle said.

Nash couldn't believe it, he thought his head was going to spin off he was so hungry. Basha picked out two dogs from the display case, along with a couple of slices of pizza, and placed them in separate boxes.

"Thank you. Come on, Nash, let's go get something to drink." Kyle said.

They went to the soda fountain. Nash got a Dr. Pepper and Kyle got a large water that they could share. After the day they had, he was sure they needed it, but he wanted Nash to drink his soda, too, if he wanted it. He felt he deserved it with everything he had been through.

They walked up and down each aisle, making sure there was nothing else that they needed. Nash ended up getting a bag of Funyuns, a pack of Twizzlers, and a KitKat.

"Geez kid, where ya puttin' all that?"

"I don't gain weight that easily. I really like sweets," Nash said with a huge grin.

"I can tell, and as far as the weight, give it another twenty years, then you'll notice it."

They walked to the counter with the food. Basha had the hot dogs and pizza waiting next to the register. Nash set the food down, trying not to stare at her, but she noticed it. She kept talking to him like he was the only person in the store. "So, is that everything?" She kept her eyes locked on Nash until he would answer.

"Uh . . . " he began. "Yeah, that's everything, I think." Then Nash looked at Kyle, seeking help.

"Yep, that's it," Kyle said, winking at Basha. He caught on to what was happening. "Hey, before I forget. Do you happen to know of a decent motel where me and my friend can stay for the night?" Kyle asked. "We're just stopping through and leaving tomorrow."

She thought for a moment. "I know there's a motel a couple miles from here, but I'm not sure what it costs. It's a Super 8."

Nash had more opportunities to look at Basha while she was distracted, talking to Kyle. He liked the way she looked.

"Will you help me find the number? Do you have a phone book?"

"Let me finish ringing this stuff up and then yes, I'll get you fixed up."

After ringing up all the items, Kyle paid while Nash started digging into his pack of Funyuns. Kyle and Basha were trying to concentrate on each other's conversation while studying the phone book, but with all the crunching going on, they couldn't help but laugh.

"What?" Nash said.

"I'm glad you're finally getting to eat, Nash."

Nash didn't know what to do. He stood there for a moment with his mouth still full. Basha smiled at him, then turned her attention back to searching for the motel. Nash was captivated. He wiped at his mouth instinctively and brushed several crumbs off his face. *Oh no! I hope I didn't look like a fool with Funyuns falling all out of me.* He dropped his head, discouraged, but kept eating.

Crunch, crunch.

"Here it is, right here," Basha said.

"Great!"

"I have a number here for a cab if you'd like me to get one for you."

"Do you mind? That would be perfect," Kyle said.

"It's no problem. You guys can hang here if you'd like and finish eating."

"Okay, thank you." Kyle looked at Nash and started gathering up their food. Nash grabbed his own drink and held a tight grip on the almost empty bag of Funyuns.

"Come on, Nash, let's sit outside on the sidewalk while we eat. Between you and your Funyuns, I don't think she wants to be cleaning up after us." Kyle rolled his eyes playfully at Basha while holding the door open for Nash.

Nash dropped his head, but saw Basha smile when he walked past, then found a new spring in his step.

They finished eating and both sat quietly for the first time in a long time not saying anything. Nash was slurping his Dr. Pepper while Kyle played with the twist top on the water bottle. It was close to nine o'clock when the cab pulled up in the parking lot. It was a generic-looking white van with the words "Checker Cab" written on both the front and passenger doors. The driver made a U-turn in the parking lot and stopped parallel with the store, the driver's door even with Kyle and Nash. Kyle gave a wave, letting the driver know they were his fare. The driver sent a flick of his fingers off the top of the steering wheel in return and threw the van into park.

Kyle gathered up the trash from the food and threw it into the garbage located next to the front entrance. Nash was already poking his head into the store, telling Basha goodbye. She was talking on the phone, but it didn't sound like a business call to Nash, more like someone she really cared about. *Maybe a boyfriend*, he thought.

"Thanks for the dogs, they were really good," Nash said, waving his hand.

"Oh, no problem. It was nice to meet you both. Be safe."

Kyle waved from the parking lot, thanking Basha for what she had done; she returned the gesture. Nash let the door close on its own weight and could swear that he heard her say, 'I can't wait to see you, too. I miss you so much.' He shook his head and walked to the van.

"It's all right, Nash, you'll find someone someday who will be just perfect for you," Kyle reassured. He opened the sliding side door of the van and Nash barreled in, immediately laying down on the bench-style seat located in the middle. Kyle slid the door shut and rode in the front seat next to the driver. Nash was already falling asleep.

* * *

When the taxi arrived at the motel, the driver stopped it at the front office, letting Kyle out to check in. He opened his door as quietly as possible without waking Nash.

"I'll be right back," he said to the driver.

The driver gave another wave with his fingers and nodded. Kyle was careful to let the door rest on its hinges, close enough to being shut without making noise. It was just enough to allow the interior light to turn off again.

The driver sat in silence with the radio tuned to some far-away AM station, barely audible. It was playing classical music. He heard Nash stir, probably because the van wasn't moving anymore. He glanced over his shoulder, but Nash was still breathing hard, keeping a steady rhythm. Then he heard the office door swing open, alerted by the little bell attached to the top of the door frame. Kyle was on his way back.

Kyle opened the sliding door of the van, leaned in, and laid a firm grip on Nash's ankle. "Nash. Nash."

Nash turned over and looked toward Kyle's voice.

"We're here, at the motel," Kyle said.

Nash stared at Kyle for a few seconds, then at the driver, trying to get his bearings. He had been in a deep enough sleep for only a couple of miles, and Kyle knew he was about to get an even better sleep if he could just get him to a bed.

"Where are we?"

"We're at the motel. Can you walk okay?"

"Yeah, sure." Nash threw his legs off the bench seat and rubbed his face. He shook his head and made a groggy sound with his voice, clearing his throat. "Okay, let's go." he said.

Kyle helped him out, then slid the door home. He closed the front passenger door as well, then walked around to the driver's door and gave him a tip. "Thanks for all your help. We really appreciate it," Kyle said, shaking the driver's hand.

"You boys be careful out there, it's a jungle." He rolled his window up and drove away.

Kyle stood for a few moments, watching the taillights get smaller. He realized that was the first and last thing the driver ever said. And the voice that came out of the man's face was not the voice that he had expected. It was too high pitched for a man that large.

Creepy.

It reminded him of the munchkins in *The Wizard of Oz.* He thought if the man's hair had been curved up into a couple of horns, the voice would have made more sense.

"Kyle? You comin'?" Nash asked, still rubbing his face with one hand. "What's the room number?"

"Oh, I'm sorry, Nash. It's room 102. Should be right up there on the left."

Nash walked across the caliche lot towards the room. There were no other cars parked close by. Most of the other guests were parked toward the U-shaped center of the lot, with rooms in the middle. He stepped over the parking curb in front of room 102 and grasped the doorknob. He hoped it would turn so he could hit the bed as soon as possible, but he knew better. He heard Kyle laugh.

"I'm coming. Here we go," Kyle said, stretching his arm out farther to reach the actual key lock. The attendant at the front desk had given him a single key attached to a florescent orange, elongated, diamond-shaped keychain, with the words "Bail Bonds" and a local number printed on it in black.

When the door opened, the air was stale, with a hint of mothballs. Nash let out a low groan of nausea, but made a B-line toward the double bed on the left side of the room, farthest from the door. There was a single lamp on, which stood on the nightstand in between the beds. Kyle shut the door and set down Nash's backpack. Having only the backpack was nice. He couldn't imagine lugging around any more than they had to.

He turned on the window unit, which was located below the front window, and set the temperature to sixty-eight degrees. He said a short prayer that the damn thing would work, because he didn't want to have to walk back to the front office. It made a few short clicks, turned on, then the constant hum leveled off to what would become relaxing. He noticed Nash was already on his bed face down and fully dressed, passed out cold, already breathing steadily again.

He took Nash's shoes off and set them at the foot of the bed. He found a couple of extra blankets on top of the rack inside the closet. He took one of them down and covered Nash, and pushed a pillow up under his head as best he could. Nash's natural reflexes took over and he adjusted himself on his side, never noticing Kyle. The other blanket ended up on Kyle's bed. He figured he would probably need it before morning, with the A/C set as low as it was. He kicked his shoes off and went to the bathroom. He washed his face, rubbing water back into his hair again to cool off. He then laid on the bed flipping channels on the remote, not really looking for anything in particular, just trying to calm down. He ended up on a classic movie channel airing a black-and-white war movie, but had the volume set so low that he would've had to turn off the A/C unit to hear it.

24

"Baboons have been getting bolder, and closer to humans than ever before," the narrator said.

Slowly waking up, Kyle could hear the television. He could feel a single bead of sweat roll across his forehead, then roll down into his left eyebrow. He realized that not only was his head sweating, but he could feel wetness over his entire body, especially his legs. He remembered just before he laid down that the room was already cooling off, and had anticipated that it would be cold when he woke. He figured that the A/C might have stopped working; maybe it burned up during the night. Now there was more reason to drag himself out of bed and get gone before anyone noticed. He wondered if Nash noticed also or if he was still out cold. *Nash!*

Kyle sat up straight, hair in a tangled web of distortion. He was staring directly at the refrigerator that was in the room. It wasn't the typical small fridge, but a full size in just a tiny room. That only made him think of one thing: water. He was extremely thirsty.

He glanced up at the television, which was still on from the night before. It was a nature documentary talking about baboons, how they sometimes enter into villages and steal human babies from their beds. There was a woman on the screen screaming in agony for the loss of her child. She happened upon the creature as it was running off, but there was nothing she could do. Kyle stared blankly at the screen, not sure what to feel; he was still trying to wake up.

He was finally able to gain his composure, and noticed that the front door was open about a quarter of the way. The sun was pouring in, sending a beam of light across the floor and up onto his bed, straight across his body. This explained the extreme heat, and on top of that, one other thing was obvious. The A/C unit was off.

When he reached over and flipped the switch to the "on" position, it responded quickly and came to life. Kyle's face tightened with curiosity. He wondered what had happened, and his thoughts turned to Nash again. He looked at Nash's bed, but he was gone. The covers had been thrown back, indicating to Kyle that Nash had become cold during the night and ended up covering himself.

Kyle was not wearing his clothes. He was only wearing his underwear, while his pants, T-shirt, and socks were all on the floor beside his bed, next to the A/C unit. He thought hard. He could not remember for the life of him when he disrobed during the night. Normally, behavior like that was when someone might drink themselves into oblivion and pass out. They get hot during the night and get undressed, then go back to bed. Maybe they even get water, or something to eat, or throw up. Regardless, they don't remember anything the next morning. This was how Kyle felt. The last thing he could recall was covering Nash with the blanket and laying down.

With one stroke, he threw the blanket, bedspread, and sheet off the rest of his body. He felt as if an extra ten pounds had been lifted from him. There was an immediate sense of relief, and the cool air that was coming out of the A/C unit felt good.

He got up and put his clothes on. He went to the bathroom and saw Nash's backpack close by. He remembered that Nash brought a few items when they left his house and could swear he brought toothpaste. He removed his blazer from the bag, and found the toothpaste in the bottom. The cold water and toothpaste were a welcoming event for Kyle. He took his time and savored the moment. There was nothing like a shower in the sink; again, washing his face, running the cool water over his head and arms. He didn't want to waste too much time actually getting in the shower. There was an obvious urgency to find Nash and get moving again. Besides, he needed to speak to him about the next step, the part he'd been dreading ever since they left Eddie.

Nash woke to the sound of a gunshot. He felt he couldn't breathe. He was laying on his stomach on the edge of the bed, looking straight at the floor. The edge of the mattress was digging into him, and he had been laying on top of his right arm, as well. When he pulled his arm out from beneath him, it felt heavy, and hurt to move. He rolled over, sat up, and watched the infomercial that was scrolling across the television screen. They were selling some new type of high-tech vacuum. There were a lot of pretty girls intentionally throwing dirt on carpets while the household pet watched. Then they would clean it up with a smile.

"That's dumb," he said to himself while trying to wiggle his fingers back to life.

He looked over at the other bed and saw Kyle bundled up under the covers. Then he remembered his dream. It was a brief dream, but quick and to the point. He was still trapped behind Kyle in the kitchen when Spencer shot some type of electric beam into his dad's skull, splintering it all across the kitchen and his own face.

The room was freezing, and he had to either turn the A/C off or go outside to warm up. The sun was already up, but it was still early. He was still in his clothes except for his shoes, but saw them sitting next to the bed. He put them on and walked over to the A/C unit and turned the knob to the off position. The sound of the motor made a whirling sound, becoming slower, then stopped. The room was almost too quiet now. He had a strong urge to eat sugar; he craved it. He remembered that he might have some loose change in the bottom of his backpack and could by a Coke from the vending machine. Most hotels had them, as far as he knew, but he had never stayed in a motel before and wasn't sure.

He found the backpack and started pulling things out, finding exactly sixty-five cents. This brought a huge smile to his face. He felt as if he had found gold. "Yes!" he said under his breath.

He opened the door carefully, trying not to make a single sound. He wanted Kyle to get all the rest he could. He knew that they would have to start walking again today or catch a cab or something. He wasn't sure what the plan was, and he was nervous about how they would end up.

He got the door open and realized it would be just as difficult to shut it. He figured it wouldn't take too long, so he left it ajar. There was a slight breeze, and he felt that would help warm the room a little.

It took him a moment or two to figure out exactly where he was. He didn't remember much after they left the flower shop, and certainly didn't remember how they got to the motel. He wondered if Kyle carried him to the room or if he walked. Surely he could remember walking, but disregarded the thought as fast as it came. In fact, he seemed to not recall a few things from the night before. He remembered playing video games, but there was a point after Kyle left to get coffee that he didn't remember. All he could recall was Eddie asking to speak to him about something, and the next thing would have been the vacuum commercial. *That thing sucked,* he thought, and made himself laugh out loud.

When he walked into the front office, there was an older man, probably in his sixties, doing some paperwork behind the counter.

"Excuse me, sir?" Nash said.

The man looked up, pulling his reading glasses a little farther down on his nose to see Nash. "Can I help you?"

"Um, yes, sir. I was wondering if you had a Coke machine on the property. I'm kinda thirsty."

The man made what Nash thought was a grunting noise and stood up. To Nash, he looked like the type of man that had done military time. The lines in his face told the whole story. He probably didn't take no for an answer and didn't like to admit he was wrong about anything. In fact, in his mind, he probably never was wrong. His lips were tight and drawn in, and the expression on his face told Nash he didn't have time to be giving directions. His hair was short and white. It was cut into a flat top. *High and tight.* That's what he had always heard. He was also big, not fat, just big. Nash guessed six four, maybe taller. Buying clothes from the store for tall and large men was a necessity for this guy.

"If you're thirsty, there's a water fountain over there," pointing to the corner next to a large Ficus tree with a television hanging above that. "If you're wanting to drink a can of sugar though, there's a machine located down the breezeway next to the janitor's closet." This time he pointed in another direction, indicating that it was outside. His fingers looked like pieces of fried cheese or cigars maybe, they were huge.

"Okay, thanks," Nash said. He turned, then stopped. "Sir? What's a breezeway?"

The man's face turned a shade of red and his lips seemed to disappear into his face, turning in such a way that his chin buckled up like a raisin. He saw the man take a deep breath and lift his finger again, pointing. "Go outside. Walk straight. Look to your left. If you've seen room 102, then you've gone too far. There's a hallway just before you get to room 102. That's a breezeway. Walk *through* there, and when you get to the end of it, you'll see the sugar dispenser." The man turned around, walked back to his desk, and sat down. He glanced at Nash, then pushed his glasses back into position.

Nash left the front office, hoping to never return. *What a tool. Guys like that need to get out more,* he thought. He tried his best to remember exactly what the man told him. "Walk straight. Look left for a hallway. No, a breezeway," he said to himself.

Nash found it exactly where the man said it would be, right next to room 102. He saw that the door was still open and could see that Kyle was still sleeping. He walked past the room into the breezeway. It seemed cooler inside the breezeway to him; being in the shade was nice and the air was rushing into his face. At the end of the breezeway was a heavenly sight to Nash. There it was in all its radiant glory, spilling a red tint across the ground, shouting the sounds of "drink me" in his mind. "All right! I found the sugar dispenser," he said to himself. "I'll have to tell Kyle about that. That's funny."

He was in luck. The price on the machine was only fifty cents, and he breathed a sigh of relief. He bought the drink and opened it. The quick release of fizz, and the sound of the pull-tab snapping the aluminum echoed throughout the breezeway. He started walking back to the room. Only the sound of his shoes connecting with the pavement could be heard bouncing off the walls around him. Nash was thrilled to know another term for hallway, "Breezeway," he said out loud, laughing a little bit. He took a long drink from the can, paused, then let out the largest belch he could, forcing it a little. It echoed loudly, and a small part of him was hoping that the man at the front desk could hear it.

"I've got your breezeway," Nash laughed.

When Nash returned to the room, the door was still open and he walked in, trying not to wake Kyle. The door pushed open without any effort and sunlight spilled into the rest of the room.

Kyle stood in the middle of the room looking at Nash. "Where were you? I was beginning to worry."

Nash jumped at the sound of his voice. He saw that Kyle was fully dressed and ready to go. Kyle looked good after their previous day together, considering the wreck, the dirt, and the blood that was shed. He looked pretty close to how he did when Nash saw him climb out of the wrecked car for the first time, except for the T-shirt under the suit jacket.

"Whoa! You scared me. I didn't think you'd be awake yet. I was getting a Coke."

"Have you been up long? It was so hot in here when I woke," Kyle said.

"Oh, I'm sorry about that. When I woke, it was freezing. I was shaking and had goose bumps and everything. The television was on, too."

"Yeah, I turned it on before falling asleep. It helps sometimes to have the noise, at least for me. I hope it didn't wake you."

"No, not at all. Anyway, I wasn't sure how to set the A/C correctly, so I turned it off until I came back," Nash said.

"It's okay. It was time for me to get up anyway. We have a busy day."

"So, what's the plan?" Nash said as he climbed up on to the bed and sat cross-legged. He set the coke can in the center where his legs crossed.

Kyle rubbed the back of his head, combing his hair with his hand along the back of his neck. He sat opposite of Nash on his own bed. "That's something I've been trying to get straight in my head ever since we left Eddie's place. And, no matter what I do, I can't seem to come up with anything better."

Nash was just finishing a drink. "Well that doesn't sound very good at all." He kept staring at Kyle, waiting for an answer.

It was an awkward silence and Kyle seemed nervous. He was rubbing his hands across the top of his legs, still thinking about how to say what he didn't want to say. This was the first time that Nash had seen him uneasy. It was hard for Kyle to make eye contact, and occasionally he would glance up at Nash.

Nash finally broke the silence. "It's okay, Kyle. I'm ready. I can take it. You're going to turn me over to the Greys right? You're going to let them go ahead and take me."

Kyle was already shaking his head, faster as Nash spoke. "No, no, no, no. That's not it at all, Nash. No way! I'm not turning you over to anyone. Well, not them at least."

Nash took another drink. "The cops?"

"No, Nash, not the cops."

"Then who? Just spit it out. I can only think of those two places that I don't want to be, so it can't be worse, can it?"

Kyle looked at Nash.

Nash was ready to hear what Kyle had to say— maybe not ready, but accepting.

"Wait a minute! You're not leaving me here, are you?" He started to stand up. "I can't stay here with that grumpy guy at the front desk!"

"Nash, Nash! Sit down, please. I'm not leaving you here."

Nash recrossed his legs and sat back down, waiting for Kyle to explain.

"Look, after everything I've told you, you understand that the Greys will never stop looking for you, right?"

Nash nodded, still listening.

"And you realize that they were looking for your father. Your mother and you were not supposed to survive, but since you *are* still alive and they never got your father, you're next."

Nash continued to listen, taking it all in. He didn't move a muscle.

"The Greys will stop at nothing to find you, and when they do, you'll never see this place again."

"What do they want me for? What do I have that's so important to them?" Nash asked.

"Your life, Nash. Your life."

Nash looked past Kyle. He looked past the curtains, past the small bit of condensation that was on the window from the A/C, and across the parking lot of the motel. He stared, trying to take it all in.

Kyle moved from his bed over to Nash's. He sat on the edge and placed one hand on Nash's knee, just at the bend. "Please try and stay with me, Nash. I need to tell you more."

Nash turned his head and looked at Kyle with lost, sad eyes. "What did I ever do to them, Kyle? What did I do?"

Kyle saw the tears starting to pool in Nash's eyes. "Nothing. You did nothing. I can't explain how they operate. They've always been here and apparently always will be. I don't know how to understand them. We may not ever understand."

"So where are you taking me? I mean, you said Eddie gave me that shot. I figured I could go with you."

"And go where, Nash?" Kyle asked. "I'm not going to have a job after all of this. I don't know what's going to happen. And, as much as I don't want to admit it, they may make me disappear." Kyle looked down, now quiet.

Nash wiped at the tears rolling down his cheeks. "Disappear?"

"Yeah, like cease to exist," Kyle said.

Nash watched Kyle. He watched his eyes as they danced back and forth, but not seeing anything at all. Nash knew he wasn't just staring at the gaudy bedspread, which was made up of different shades of orange and light blue patches. It was something straight from the 70s. "Kyle?" Nash said in between his sniffles.

Kyle finally looked up. "I guess I drifted off. Sorry." He readjusted his position on the edge of the bed, now with both feet on the floor, looking out the same window Nash had been. "I feel bad, Nash. I hope I haven't upset you."

"No, of course not. I want you to be safe too," Nash said.

Kyle smiled. "There's a place that I know of where you will be well taken care of and can start a new life."

Nash listened, but was unsure of what to think. He felt his emotions being torn every which way and didn't know what to feel. Just a little over twenty-four hours ago, this man was not considered a friend. He was a murderer, along with his partner. Now, by some miraculous turn of events, he felt close to Kyle and trusted him. His mother crossed his mind again, and the tears started. "What kind of place, Kyle?"

"It's called Skyward Dude Ranch. It's a place where children go when they don't have a home," Kyle said.

This made Nash break down more as he was reminded of being truly homeless. "You mean I'll be an orphan." Nash dropped his head. He played with the top of the soda can. His eyes were red and puffy from crying. He continued wiping at his nose, trying to make it stop running. "I know what orphans are. I heard my dad talking to my mom about orphans one time. I'm not sure if it was about me or not."

Kyle grabbed the roll of toilet paper from the restroom and brought it back to Nash.

"It's okay, Nash. Places like the ranch have good people. They'll help you finish school, and you would make all sorts of new friends. Plus, one day, you might be able to start a new family."

Nash wiped his nose with the paper and the tears were starting to subside. "New family? With who? You mean married?"

"No, you could get adopted, that's what I mean." Kyle said.

"A new set of parents? Don't fool yourself, I'm sixteen years old. Nobody's going to adopt someone my age."

"You can't say that, Nash. Everyone needs a home and you never know who or what opportunity is going to walk through that door."

"I wish I could stay with you. You're probably the only person I trust now. Isn't that strange?" Nash said.

Kyle looked at Nash and couldn't help but smile. He knew he hadn't done right by Nash overall and couldn't believe what he was hearing. Nash had been through so much, but still found trust deep within, somewhere. Kyle wished at that moment he could hold Nash up for everyone in the world to see, to use him as an example, to show them how humanity was supposed to be. This person was real and forgiving. "Yes, I am surprised to hear you say that after everything we've been through, and I also want to say thank you."

"For what?" Nash said.

"For trusting me. But you do still understand why you can't stay with me, right? I mean, there's no telling what's going to happen to me. I need to get you safe and continue on my own."

"Where will you go?" Nash asked.

"I'm not sure. I may just go to Terminus X. I can't keep running. They'll eventually find me."

"You can't give up, Kyle, you have to at least try. Maybe you should have taken the shot like me, just in case."

This gave Kyle second thoughts. He knew he had protected the fact that his tooth was a tracking device and no one else knew, but now his mind was messing with him. *I wonder if someone had planted another device on me without me knowing?* He shrugged the thought away. "I'm going to be fine, Nash, but I need you to do this. I promise you'll be happier once things calm down and you get in a routine. It's best for you."

Nash was still rubbing his fingers along the top of the soda can. His voice was still weak from crying. "I'd rather tag along with you."

Kyle put his hand on Nash's head and pulled him in close, giving him a hug. "I'm so sorry about every bit of this. Please trust me one last time and let's get you safe."

Nash hugged Kyle back, then wiped his eyes one last time. "I trust you, Kyle, I really do. I know you're right also, and that I should go."

Kyle patted Nash on the back. He was happy for him. "You should get your things together. We need to get going. We don't want to get charged for another day's stay. The guy that works at the front counter is a little odd."

"He's a tool! I figured that out when I went to go buy this Coke. He got all bent out of shape because I didn't know what a breezeway was." Nash scoffed. He finished the drink and set it on the nightstand.

"Do you?" Kyle asked.

"I do now."

"So you didn't know?"

"No, not really. He even started turning red when I asked. To me it sounded like a word someone would use if they were having gas problems or constipation."

"Oh God!" Kyle shouted. "That's gross! Where'd you get your sense of humor?"

"I don't know, probably my mom. My dad's kinda serious."

Kyle had really taken a liking to Nash. He promised himself right then that if there was some way he could get out of this whole mess, he would come back and find him again, at least check on him when he could.

"How far is it to this ranch place, Kyle?"

"It's not that far, actually. I looked it up last night after we got here. Looks like it's only about a twenty minute drive, but by foot it could take a while. So we definitely need to catch a ride."

* * *

They left the room and went to the lobby. They were in luck, because the man working earlier was not around. A woman had taken his place, at least for the time being. She assisted them with checking out and helped Kyle arrange for a taxi. Kyle noticed the wedding ring on her hand and assumed she was more than likely the wife of the older gentleman, but he didn't ask. She had a pleasantness about her that drew Kyle and Nash in. Everything she did seemed to flow from some other place, a place of peace and grace, and they both sensed it.

They finished checking out and decided to sit outside on the curb and wait, especially after hearing the woman talking to someone in the back of the office. They figured the husband was back and neither one of them wanted any part of that.

Kyle noticed that Nash was a little more quiet than usual. "Nash? You okay?"

"Yeah, I think so. Why?"

"You look like you've got something on your mind that's all."

Nash sat with his thumbs propped behind the straps of his backpack, looking across the open highway. There wasn't much to look at other than the empty field that would probably be developed soon, being this close to town. They had only traveled a couple of miles from the 7-11 the night before, and the motel was located off the highway going west, back out of town. "I'm thinking of my mother from time to time."

"Well, I'm sure she was a good mom to you. She seemed very considerate and nice when I met her," Kyle said.

"Yeah, she was always that way with everyone. She seemed to always put other people's needs ahead of hers."

Kyle didn't say anything, just an occasional nod. He felt even worse for what happened to Nash's mother. Why couldn't she have been a loser, maybe a junkie who treated her son like shit? *No, you had to end up on the assignment where you took an innocent boy from his saint-like mother.* "I'm sorry, Nash. I am, really, about everything."

Nash showed no expression and nodded. His eyes seemed distant to Kyle. "Are you sure you're okay?" Kyle asked.

"I wasn't sure and didn't want to make you nervous, but my head is starting to hurt a little bit," Nash said.

Kyle wasn't sure what to do. He looked at Nash. "Now? What should we do? What should I do?"

"Nothing. There's nothing to do; it will pass. I promise, it won't last long," Nash said.

There was a moment of silence between them, but Kyle didn't want to press the issue any more than necessary. He kept a close eye on Nash, watching and listening for anything out of the ordinary. He watched the road, with an occasional car driving by. Each person that drove by couldn't help but look at the two of them sitting so close to the road, probably wondering what they were doing. Kyle realized that it was simple human nature to instinctively slow down and stare at something on the side of the road, regardless of what was going on behind or ahead of you. He was thankful they were not in the city or there would probably be a traffic jam, with them being the subject of a full-fledged gawkers block. The last thing they needed was more attention. He was starting to feel anxiety build inside him. Then he felt his heart skip a beat at the sound of a horn.

The taxi was just pulling off the main road into the caliche, and stopped ten feet shy of them. Nash looked to his left and saw another minivan like the night before and was now staring directly at the grill of the van. A not-so-fortunate grasshopper stared back at him. Its legs were twisted in the opposite direction, laying across where the head should have been. Nash continued his emotionless stare at the creature, lost somewhere in between here and a dream.

Kyle stood up and waved to the driver, who was barely visible. The sun was just right in the sky, creating a glare across the dirty windshield. All he could pick out was that the driver was wearing glasses, which had a glare on them also, and a cowboy hat.

"Nash, come on," Kyle said.

Nash continued to stare at the grasshopper for at least another minute, then finally stood up. He kept his eyes on the dead grasshopper while fumbling with his backpack, straightening it on his back. He finally looked away, finding Kyle waiting beside him.

"You ready?"

"Yeah, let's go," Nash said. He walked past Kyle to the side of the van. He opened the sliding door and got in, finding himself a nice spot so he could spread out a little bit.

Kyle glanced down at the grasshopper with squinted eyes; the sun was now bouncing off the chrome bumper. He looked at it, trying to figure out if Nash was seeing something he wasn't. He scoffed and got in the front passenger seat.

"You fellas ready?" the driver said.

Kyle pulled out a piece of stationary on which he had written the address to the Skyward Dude Ranch and handed it to the driver. "Do you know this place?"

The driver was a young male, fair skinned, with jet-black hair sticking out from underneath his cowboy hat. He was thin and wore a plain white T-shirt tucked into a pair of faded jeans, along with worn cowboy boots. He spoke with a northern accent. Kyle wanted to think it was a New York accent, but wasn't positive. He seemed to drift from north to south, like he was slipping in and out of character.

The driver looked at the address inquisitively, then confirmed with Kyle. "I know this place. You want to go here?"

"Yeah, to that place," Kyle said, pointing at the paper.

"Okay, mister. You're the boss." The driver folded the paper once and set it in a small compartment recessed into the dash, below the radio. He put the van into drive and hit the accelerator. It was a little too hard at first, causing the back tires to spin on the loose ground beneath them. He let off abruptly, then started again, this time easier.

Kyle watched out for other traffic. He felt more anxious the longer Nash was with him, the closer the time came to the gathering, to Terminus X. He thought someone would have found him by now and killed him and taken Nash, but still nothing. He considered the shot that Eddie gave Nash. *Did it actually work? Why doesn't Nash seem to remember it? Is that the memory loss Eddie mentioned?*

He could only hope that it had worked. If he could get the boy settled in, and go, distance himself. He could at least feel calm that Nash was going to be okay, and get a second chance at life. Then it was a matter of figuring out the best course for himself. He knew, in the end, he was dead. And, for the first time, he questioned his actions when he was with Spencer back at the farm. If he had gone along with him and delivered Nash, this would be over. He would be making arrangements to meet at Terminus X with the boy and start a new assignment the following day, clean and simple. But deep down in his gut, he knew he had done the right thing. Thoughts of his brother were eating at him, wanting to find him, or at least get some more answers on what had happened.

Kyle looked back at Nash, who was sleeping again. Then it hit Kyle. *Did he just have one of those blackouts he told me about?* He wasn't sure. He had to watch Nash's chest for a moment to make sure he was breathing. He turned back around to watch the road, hoping Nash might have some answers when he woke up. He also hoped and prayed that Nash would have a future to look forward to.

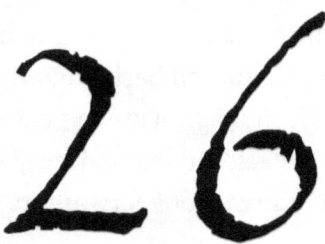

"There she is," the driver said.

Nash heard this and raised his head. He looked out the window and saw the Skyward Dude Ranch. *Is this the place where I'm supposed to live from now on, until someone comes along and wants to take care of me, if at all?* He thought of these things as he studied the grounds. There was the main part of the building, which actually was a mansion. It was mainly white, with a large wrap-around-style porch. The roof was Spanish-style with large red clay tiles overlapping one another. He noticed a porch swing on one side near the front door. To the right of the mansion was a large playground with all types of activities for younger children. There were seesaws and slides, even some spring riders in different animal shapes. Then the playground seemed to grow as the van turned into the driveway toward the entrance. He saw a castle with more than enough hiding places for kids to have all sorts of different adventures, a slide that came out of a dragon's mouth, and a large gargoyle statue that was the entrance to a bridge that crossed over to a swing set. Nash couldn't stand it any longer.

"Are you kidding me? Look at this place!"

"Well, that was fast. You seem to be acting more like yourself," Kyle said.

"Is this really the place, Kyle? It's huge."

"This is the place."

"This ain't the half of it kid," the driver said. "There's more on the other side and out back. Wait until you see the swimming pool."

Nash and Kyle both listened to the driver while they peered out of the window of the van. Nash couldn't believe what he was seeing, and felt happiness that he never thought he would find again.

"Do you skateboard?" the driver asked.

"No, but it sounds fun," Nash said.

"Well, if you ever want to learn or like to watch, there's a skateboard park built out back. There are some pretty talented kids here, you won't believe it."

"This place is amazing, Kyle," Nash said as he hung between the front seats, one hand on each of the headrests.

"It is a great place, and you'll meet a lot of people. Shoot, don't ever worry, because even if a family doesn't come along for you, these people will always be your family. I should know. I used to live here."

"Did you really?" Kyle asked.

"Yes, sir. I lived here for roughly five years when I was younger, a little younger than your friend here."

Nash held out his hand. "My name's Nash."

"Name's Tim."

Nash looked him over once and realized that Tim was a very small individual, not small, but very thin.

Kyle offered his hand. "Kyle, nice to meet you."

Nash couldn't stand it any longer and jumped out of the van, sliding the door closed behind him. He started walking toward the playground but stopped, observing from where he was and taking it all in.

"I don't want to get too personal and mean no disrespect, but are you checking him in here? Dropping off?" the driver asked..

"Yes, I'll be checking him in. I'm his uncle," Kyle said.

"Gotcha. Well, I don't mean to pry, but I'm assuming you'll need a ride out of here after he's all settled in. Here's my card, let me know when you're all finished up and I'll come back. I need to run into town and put some more gas in this thing, maybe grab me a bite to eat."

"That sounds good, thank you," Kyle said.

"Just call me direct when you're ready. That's my cell number."

"Thanks, Tim," Kyle said, holding the card and showing good faith by putting it in his front breast pocket. He got out of the van and shut the door.

Tim raised two fingers to the side of his head, waving a salute, and drove away.

* * *

They walked past the porch swing and Nash gave one of the chains a slight flick of his finger, making the chain vibrate like the string on a guitar. The weight of the swing pulled tight, however, the tone was too low to hear; it just vibrated, and the reverberations could be seen in the movement of the swing.

Kyle turned the doorknob and walked inside. Nash followed, still excited about being at the ranch. Once inside, they stopped near a large wooden desk. It had a small lamp on it, lighting up a portion of the desk with miscellaneous paperwork stacked neatly. In the middle of the desk, there was a small, plastic container with a half-eaten salad, and a fork still buried deep in the leaves of lettuce. Next to it was a can of diet soda.

Kyle didn't pay too much attention other than the fact that someone was in the middle of eating and left. On the outer edge of the desk was a Newton's Cradle. Nash saw it and couldn't resist. He grabbed one of the metal balls and let it go.

"I love these things, Kyle," he said, giggling to himself.

Tap, tap, tap, tap, the metal balls screamed throughout the empty room. They continued to pierce into Kyle's head as he scanned the room. It was very quiet, almost too quiet for him. "Where is everyone?" There was no one in the main room at all, and he couldn't hear anyone talking in any other part of the house close by. He laid one hand upon the Newton's Cradle, stopping the metal balls from crashing together.

Nash stopped smiling and looked around. "Wow, Kyle, it's quiet in here. Where is everyone?"

"I'm not sure, Nash, but you would think that we could hear something."

"Wait a sec. I do hear some music playing," Nash said.

Kyle tilted his head toward the ceiling and was able to pick up a tune coming from the speakers recessed into the ceiling. It was "Boogie Shoes" by KC and the Sunshine Band, singing their silly little hearts out. Now that Nash mentioned it, it seemed louder. When no one was in the building talking, without regular everyday activities going on, the music was very audible. "That's a good song. Have you ever heard it?"

"No, why?" Nash said.

"Something doesn't seem right to me here, and if things don't improve, we may have to boogie right on outta here," Kyle explained.

Nash swallowed hard and looked around; he was beginning to perspire.

"Let's go this way, Nash. We have to look around and find someone. Maybe this is just a coincidence. Maybe they're all together somewhere having a meeting or something."

Nash followed Kyle as they made their way past the reception desk and a visiting area, which had a small coffee table, couch, and two chairs. In between the two chairs was a table with a lamp and a few magazines. On the coffee table was a large arrangement of flowers; the scent filled the room. Nash loved looking at them and especially loved the smell. That's when he noticed the card still attached to one of the stems. It twisted in the air slowly from the breeze escaping from one of the A/C vents in the room. Nash was almost positive he recognized the name. When the card turned again, he saw "Floral Design Boutique."

"Hey," he began.

Kyle stopped. "What? You hear something?"

He wasn't sure why, but he stopped himself. "Well, I thought I did. Never mind. I guess it was nothing."

Kyle continued walking and came to an intersection. The hallway was lit up bright to the left, but dimmer to the right, with a faint light coming from underneath the first door on the left. "Nash?"

"Yeah."

"Why don't you take a left here and start looking into these rooms. Call me if you see or find anyone. I'll go this way. If I see something I'll call you."

Nash's voice shook. "Um, okay."

Kyle nodded and went right. Nash watched Kyle walk away, then turned back toward his part of the hallway. The music was not much fun anymore. He could hear it, but he wished he could yank the cord out of the wall and unplug the stupid thing. He never wanted to hear KC and the fuck sticks anymore, as long as he lived in fact. This was nerve wracking. "I was so excited just a few minutes ago.

Why do I feel like I'm in a haunted house now?" he mumbled to himself.

"Did you say something, Nash?"

"No. I mean yes. I'm singing along to the music, Kyle."

"Okay."

The closer Kyle got to the door, the more he could smell something. There was something cooking close by. The door wasn't completely shut. He pushed on it easily. It opened without a sound, stopping just shy of a bread rack behind the door. It was a large kitchen area, what you might see in a hotel. Everything was stainless steel with professional, top-notch appliances. There were several cooking utensils on the island in the middle and a few bowls out with prepped food waiting, but waiting for who was the question. There was a large pot on the stove, along with a flame underneath on low.

He walked closer to the island and could see some of the prepped food a little better. There were small bowls with different items in each. He was definitely no chef and never intended on trying to be one; he was better at eating. But even though he was not a cook, he knew enough that the food waiting on the island was to be added to the pot on the stove, but whoever was supposed to do that was missing also.

KC and the Sunshine Band finished doing their thing, and Maxine Nightingale started in with "Right Back Where We Started."

Kyle let out a sigh. "More disco. What kind of place is this, after all?"

He walked over to the stove and touched the top of the lid on the pot very fast, testing to see if it was too hot. He did it again, then again, making sure it was okay to lift the lid. He was dying to see and smell this first-hand. He grasped the top and pulled.

27

"Kyle!! Kyle!! Get down here quick!" Nash yelled.

Kyle ran out of the kitchen, letting the door swing open enough to rattle the bread rack behind the door. Once in the hall, he could see Nash standing at the opposite end shaking his head and staring at something.

"What's wrong with them, Kyle? What's wrong with them?" He could hear Nash saying as he got closer. He could tell that he was on the verge of tears the way he was speaking.

He stopped running a few feet away from Nash and began to walk. He was very hesitant to see what was in the room, but assumed the worst. He approached Nash, still looking at him.

Nash looked at Kyle with fear in his eyes, "What's wrong with them, Kyle?"

Kyle gathered his courage and slowly turned his attention to the open door leading into a large conference room.

* * *

What Kyle saw next was nothing he could have ever been prepared for. He expected in his heart to see a dead body or even several dead bodies. Somehow, and he wasn't sure how, this was worse.

He slowly walked into the room looking left and right, making sure there was nothing that would be behind him after entering. They were all there. Men, women, and children lined the walls. They were sitting on the floor, some hand in hand, some with children sitting in their laps. Loved ones grasped one another tight. They started on one side of the room, to his right, all along the wall making a semi-circle to the other side of the room, ending on his left. Then it seemed to start again in the middle of the room in rows. Rows of people of all ages, mostly kids under the age of twenty-one, filled the room like an outdoor concert. They were all facing him. Everyone was staring directly at him, or staring at whoever once stood in his spot. These people were in some sort of suspended animation. Some had looks of fear and dread, some sad, and some showed no signs of struggle or stress. They had all been looking at someone, or some *thing*, when whatever occurred to them happened.

"Jesus." Kyle whispered. He couldn't stand there too long. Whether they were aware or not, Kyle was unable to stand there with every pair of eyes on him, watching. He looked away. He walked through the first couple of rows of people, and brushing up against someone from time to time sent chills through him. One time he stepped on someone's hand who happen to have it on the floor at the time of paralysis. "I'm sorry. I'm so sorry," he said, bending down toward that person so they really knew he was sorry. The hand had turned red and looked like it hurt, but the person never moved and the expression never changed.

Once in the midst of the people, he turned and faced in the direction they were all looking, trying to figure out what they might have seen or what they might have been doing at that moment. He couldn't block the feelings from his mind anymore. No matter how many different scenarios or excuses he came up with, he always came back to the truth. He knew exactly what had been going on here, and he knew exactly what was going to happen next, no matter what. He figured it was just a matter of time before he was caught. For all he knew, he was being followed the whole time. He was sure of it. The Grey's had found him. He still wasn't sure about Nash, but he knew they had somehow tracked him here, to this moment.

"Kyle?" Nash said. "Are you okay?" He stood outside the door looking in, but didn't want to walk in.

"Yeah, Nash, I'm fine. But, we need to talk."

"Okay. I don't wanna walk in there, Kyle. Could you come out here?" Nash said with his head down. He couldn't look into the room any more. The people staring back at him were unbearable.

"Yeah, hang on. I'm coming."

Nash stood in the hallway, backpack still in place, wringing his hands together. Kyle stepped into the hallway and placed a hand on Nash's shoulder. Nash jumped.

"Whoa, I'm sorry, Nash. It's okay."

"That's all right. Now what, Kyle? What happened to them?"

"Well, I'm afraid I owe you an apology. I think both of us knew deep down that this day might come, but I know that we both dreamed that it wouldn't."

"What are you talking about, Kyle?"

Kyle started walking down the hall, heading back toward the front of the building. Nash followed, listening. "I guess you remember when I took the tracker out of my mouth back at your parent's house, right?"

Nash thought. "Yeah, I remember, of course. It looked like it hurt real bad."

"It did, but that's not the point. The point is, Nash, I messed up. I think I told you that it's possible that they might still find us. Now that you've taken the shot from Eddie, now I guess it's just me that they've found."

"They? Who's they? What are you trying to say, Kyle?" Nash said, grasping both straps of his backpack, letting his shoulders hang.

Kyle took in a long breath and exhaled deeply. He did not want to hurt Nash. It wasn't supposed to happen this way. "The Greys," Kyle said.

"Them? The little green men? They're here? Now?" Nash started looking around frantically, then started walking faster toward the main lobby. Kyle followed quickly, catching up to Nash.

"We have to stay calm, Nash. We have to figure this out together."

"Are you crazy, Kyle? I don't wanna be here. I have to get outta here. I'm not going into space. I'm not going to end up cut open somewhere on some operating table."

"Nash!" Kyle yelled. He grabbed Nash by the backpack, swinging him around.

"You have to stay calm, Nash. You need to listen to me."

Kyle had both hands on Nash's shoulders, trying to explain the best way out of this mess.

"Look. You're protected. They don't know you're here, only me. I'm the one they tracked, and now all of those people in the next room are in danger also."

"What do you mean? Are they dead?

"No, not yet at least. They've been marked and will be gathered later, probably tonight."

"You mean at Terminus X, right?"

"That's right."

"Well, maybe we should leave then, so when they come back to take them to the gathering we'll be gone. I don't want to be caught. I don't want to go to Terminus X," Nash explained.

"Nash. This *is* Terminus X."

Nash's face went pale and his knees buckled.

Kyle pulled Nash in close. "When they come back, they won't be alone. There will be a lot of them, and a lot of people being taken. They won't miss anyone."

"No!!! We've come so far! I don't want to die! You promised!"

"What I promised was to get you a better life and to keep you safe from being taken, and I still intend to do that," Kyle said. "So, the way that we do that is to get you out of here. You need to go, Nash."

Nash stood back and looked at the door. "You're not coming, are you?"

"I can't. If they've tracked me here, then they'll track me anywhere. Those people in the next room. I've seen it before and it's no joke. They're ready to be gathered and there's nothing I can do for them. The Greys are the only ones that can reverse it, and believe me, they won't. I have to stay here, Nash. They're after me."

"What are you talking about? You're going to give up? Give yourself to them? Where am I supposed to go?" Nash asked.

"Get out of town, Nash. Find another orphanage and start over. Tell them you don't have a family. Don't try and do this alone; find help after I'm gone. It's the only way."

"I'm scared, Kyle. I don't want to leave."

"I am too, but it's time." Kyle walked Nash to the door, neither one of them speaking. Nash was still in disbelief, and looked at Kyle from time to time, shaking his head. He was lost, no choice or knowledge of what to do. His thoughts went to his mother again. He wanted to go home and start over, to start differently. He wanted a new family now. He wanted to be different, to be better, and at that moment, smarter.

They reached the door and paused.

"I promise, Nash, this is the best way. You need to get as far from here as possible. Just go. But I beg you, please, don't do this alone. Find help. Find your way. You can do it."

Nash nodded, then hugged Kyle around the waist. "Thank you for helping me," Nash said.

Kyle teared up and wrapped his arms around Nash. "No problem, kid. You stay strong." He held onto him for a few moments, which seemed an eternity to Kyle. His mind raced about what to do next. He had no idea when the Greys would be back and couldn't take the chance of them catching Nash with him. He pulled away. "Go, it's time."

Kyle grabbed the doorknob.

28

The smell of flesh filled the air and Nash's nose crinkled up, the stench making him gag. Kyle, still holding onto the doorknob, realized he could not let go. It was burning his hand, and he was unable to turn it. Nash watched Kyle start to convulse. He stepped back and charged at Kyle, pushing as hard as he could, knocking him loose.

They hit the floor with Nash tripping and landing on top of him. Kyle's hand continued to smoke, and was red with third-degree burns. He screamed out in pain. "Son of a bitch! Damn!"

Nash couldn't help but stare at the burnt hand. He wanted to help somehow but wasn't sure what to do. "Kyle? What do I do? What can I do?"

"Nothing, nothing. I'll be fine. They're here. We gotta get you out of here." Kyle got to his feet and ran to the windows in the main living area. He tried both sets of windows, but nothing. They wouldn't budge. The windows were unlocked and normally free to slide open, but were unmovable. He went to the next set of windows in the same room on the adjacent side—same thing, nothing.

Nash tried another set on the opposite wall. "Kyle! These won't open either. What's wrong with them?"

"Not sure! Try the other room opposite the hallway."

Nash ran to the next room while Kyle crossed through the main entry in the room with the small coffee table. There was a single window there. It was sealed tight also. He knew they were trapped. The Greys were here, and they were running the show.

"What do you want from me?! I'm here! Come on!" Kyle yelled. He eased his hand into the inside coat pocket of his blazer. The fabric rubbed his burned hand and made him wince in pain. He continued. He was reaching for the one thing that he still had from the day they took Destry's house; the day he killed Spencer. He had the gun. He never told Nash that he still had it. He wasn't sure what Nash would do, or if it would push him over the edge mentally seeing the same gun that killed his father. The gun itself was fashioned in such a way that with a couple of turns, it could be condensed into a small singular piece of metal and hidden almost anywhere. It was about the size of a Zippo lighter. But, at this particular moment, his pocket was empty.

He removed his hand from his pocket and looked around frantically. He couldn't imagine where the gun had gone. He had had it the entire time and never recalled losing track of it. This was the one thing he needed right then. Thoughts raced through his head, trying to replay the past two or three days in his mind; the room became darker.

He looked out of the windows and noticed the clouds thickening and the skies turning black. The wind was picking up and he could see the trees starting to bend, swaying hard. The grass in front of the dude ranch was blown over, completely flat.

He grabbed the small chair to his right and threw it at the window, trying to break through. The chair bounced off of the glass like rubber and caught Kyle in the left forearm when he tried to block his face. He screamed out. "Come on! Fight me face-to-face if you want me. Stop screwing around!"

275

The wind stopped. The trees were still. It was silent again, but the skies were still black. He could see something in the sky above the house, but obscure. He couldn't quite make it out, but he knew what it was. The Greys.

"Nash!" he yelled. He could see movement outside of the windows. *People?* No, they were too small, and they were multiplying. No matter which window he looked out, the number of them was growing. They were surrounding the house. Then he noticed the trucks. Several military vehicles pulled up in front of the dude ranch, red and blue lights flashing in all directions. He could hear the sound of soldiers, now on the ground, surrounding the place and securing all exits.

"Nash!" Kyle yelled.

"Nash isn't here right now, Kyle, but I'll talk to you."

Kyle turned and saw Nash standing behind him, at least it was Nash's body. However, the look on his face, wasn't Nash's. This was a different person, someone who had been around for a long time. He could see it in the eyes. They were bright blue, and wise, much more in the moment than Nash could have ever been. But it was confusing for Kyle to look at him. All he could see was Nash standing there, but he knew better.

"Who are you?"

"Kyle. You were always the smart one, not Spencer. He was so angry, all the time it seemed, so uptight."

"Not angry, cautious," Kyle explained.

"Yes, cautious. I'll agree with you on that."

"Good. Now what?" Kyle said. "What do I call you? Nash Jr.?"

The being smiled. "No, of course not. How about Quick?"

Kyle felt the hair stand on his neck and the terror start to move within him. "I can't say it's good to see you again, Quick."

"Are you looking for this?" He held out his hand, and there in the center of his palm was the gun that Kyle had been searching for. Quick made a fist around the piece of metal and moved his fingers in such a way that the metal transformed rapidly into the shape that Kyle could only hope to have in his own grasp at that moment. He pointed it at Kyle. "I love these things. The weapons division was always my favorite. This one is perfect." Quick said.

Kyle felt the air change around him. His hair was actually starting to stand, and the air seemed drier. He could hear a high-pitched tone winding up, like a jet engine, but faint. The gun had been engaged. "So, you just gonna shoot me? Is that it?"

"We can talk for a few minutes if you'd like. We don't have to leave just yet. Besides, not everyone has been loaded on board. What would you like to talk about?" Quick disengaged the gun. It disassembled back into its smaller state, and he slid it away in his front pocket. He folded his hands in front of him, like a man waiting on a bus. He stared at Kyle with that same casual smile.

"First of all, where's Nash? How is this possible?"

"Nash is here. He's always been here. I am simply borrowing him, if you will."

"For you to be able to do that, you would have had to have a tracker on him," Kyle said.

"Very good," Quick said, clapping his hands together. "See, you are the smart one, Kyle."

"Stop your bullshit, Quick! What's going on? Quit jerking me off and tell me how."

"We've been with you ever since you found Nash," Quick said. "Is that what you want to hear? Is that plain enough for you? In fact, we were with Nash soon after his very first breath of life."

"What? No, you're lying," Kyle said.

"I'm afraid not. Yes, someone had to help us keep an eye on Destry. The man was a wreck. It was just a matter of time before he starting singing like a bird about what he saw. That's when you and your Spencer showed up to save the day. We wanted Destry, but that plan didn't work out so well now did it?"

"That's not possible. Eddie. The shot," Kyle said.

Quick starting laughing to himself. "Eddie. Poor guy. He must be completely troubled by all of this. I will have to send my apologies, maybe, someday."

"What'd you do? What do you mean? Nash got the shot to kill the tracker, if he had one," Kyle said.

"Oh! Obviously he had one, but a shot he did not receive," Quick said. "Eddie, on the other hand, did receive a shot. I don't believe he liked it, though. Once you came back, he wanted us to leave rather quickly, if you recall," Quick smiled again.

"Son of a bitch, no wonder he wanted us to leave so fast. You *have* been here the whole time, controlling Nash. Is he even real?"

"Oh he's real, and all of his emotions are his. He is his own person, but when I want to intervene, I do. He is temporarily—how would you say?—put on pause would be the best way to say it, I guess."

"Is Eddie going to die?" Kyle asked.

"Oh come on, Kyle, it was just a shot. No. He'll be fine. I'm sure he was sore for a while, mentally and physically, but I'm sure he's over it by now. He was right. The serum was to dissolve the tracking device, that's all. It didn't harm him, if that comforts you to know."

"Yes, it does. Thank you," Kyle said.

Quick looked surprised at Kyle's response.

They both stood in silence for a moment, Kyle played out anything and everything he could do. Realizing now that Nash had been a host for the Greys the entire time turned his stomach, but at the same time, he couldn't help but think, *well played*. And Eddie, he wished he could see Eddie right now to tell him he was sorry for all the trouble and thank him for all that he tried to do.

"What's the next move, Quick?" Kyle said.

"For all that you've done, killing your own partner, an agent no doubt, and attempting to hide a known recruit for the cause, well that, my friend, is death."

"A known recruit for the cause? Who? Nash?"

Quick nodded.

"You've got to be kidding me! Nash was supposed to die along with his mother and you were to take the father. That much I do know."

"Looks like things changed after you left with the boy. He then became a recruit of interest."

Kyle laughed. "Ha! A recruit of interest. Well, that's just great. Here I was walking around with a kid that I thought was technically dead to The Corporation, and you guys."

"He's needed for the cause now. He's proven to be quite useful to us," Quick said.

Kyle looked around the room, praying for the right words to come to him. He still wanted to fight for Nash. At first he thought Nash was a made-up person, a Grey through and through, but knowing that they'd just been controlling him gave Kyle hope. Nash could still lead his own life if he could convince them to leave him alone, to leave him on Earth. "What about all the other people in the next room? What's going to happen to them?"

"They're part of this too. You've been with The Corporation for some time now. I recall seeing you at Terminus X before. I do believe you know how this works."

"I wondered if they were actually being taken, or if that was just to secure the structure until you left. I figured you might free them," Kyle said.

Quick laughed. "You've still got some fight in you, don't you? I like that. Wait a minute, this is about your brother, isn't it? You're still upset."

"David? I guess deep down it's always been about him. You ripped him from our lives, my life! He could have been great. But no! You had to take him. You have to take them all and cut them open! Experiment on them or who knows what!"

Quick, still shaking his head with a look of empathy. "Kyle. Would you like to speak to David? There is so much you don't understand."

Kyle stood holding his hand, cradling it, looking around for anyone that might be coming from the sides or behind him. He could still see other Greys moving about outside, along with soldiers holding their positions with weapons drawn. "I'm not an idiot, Quick. I know he's gone, dead, whatever. Please don't do that to me, no head games."

"This isn't a game, Kyle. If you would like to speak with him, you can, right now. Just as I'm talking to you now through Nash, David can also, and I will not interfere. It might do you some good."

Kyle watched as Quick lost his facial expression and looked very distant, but only for a few seconds. His eyes blinked and he looked around, gathering his surroundings. He looked at Kyle.

"Kyle? Is that you?" The voice coming out of Nash's body was not Nash's, and had taken a different tone than that of Quick. It was a young, more innocent-sounding voice.

"Well, yeah it's me. I'm still here. I'm . . . " Kyle stopped himself and realized the voice was different and looked closely at Quick, trying to understand. "David?"

"Kyle. It is you. It's me, David." David smiled, eyes shining brightly at his brother.

Kyle's knees buckled, and he began to cry. "David?" He started to walk toward him. He wanted to take him in his arms and squeeze tight and never let go. After a few steps, he stopped.

David held one hand out. "You shouldn't. But do trust that it's me."

Through tears, Kyle said, "I believe you. I can tell by your eyes and expression." Kyle wiped the tears from underneath his eyes with his good hand. "How are you? I have so much to ask, things I wonder about. I thought you were dead. How is this possible?"

David smiled, watching his brother. "You look the same, Kyle. Well, older," David winked.

"Ha! I'll be damned," Kyle said. "This is unbelievable."

"Kyle, there is so much to say, but as you've probably gathered, there isn't time. I'm allowed to tell you the specifics, to help you understand."

Kyle nodded and listened. He took one more step forward, still holding his other hand.

David took a step forward also. "Kyle, to ease your mind, the people who are taken are not killed or tortured. This has been a misconception since the beginning. Everyone who is taken serves a purpose. There is so much going on in this universe that too many people wouldn't understand, or couldn't understand. It's too much to take in."

Kyle's tears had dried, and he listened intently, staring deeply into David. "What kind of purpose? What do you do?"

"We protect this planet and make plans for future generations. Someday this planet will become unstable and things will change again."

"Relocation?" Kyle asked.

David nodded. "There's always a plan in motion and the survival of the human race is important not only to the humans, but to all."

"The government knows all of this too?"

"The government knows portions. They know enough to keep information from the people of Earth, and they know enough to still desire the technological information we can give them in exchange for what we do."

Kyle looked at his surroundings. He glanced out one of the windows to find a few pairs of bulbous eyes peering in, and the object in the sky still hovering above the house, then turned back to David. He nodded. "This is amazing that I'm talking to you. You may not look like yourself, but I know it's you. Thank you for seeing me."

"I've wanted to do this also, but didn't know if it would ever be possible. I am thankful."

"I don't want to die, David. They're going to kill me for what I did. Can you help me?"

"You're a good man, Kyle, with a huge heart. You took a liking to Nash, and even though your intentions were good, your actions getting to this point were not," David explained.

"Can you help me save Nash? I want to fulfill my promise to him. He needs to live a real life; he has nothing left. Take *me* away if you have to; let me come with you. Show me this cause. I'll help. Please let him live a long life. He's been through enough," Kyle pleaded.

"I have to go, Kyle. It's been wonderful speaking with you again. I love you." David's face faded and turned solemn.

Kyle stared at David. "David? David, come back!"

Quick's eyes blinked and looked at Kyle. Kyle took a few steps back, grasping his burned hand.

"Did you enjoy seeing your brother?" Quick asked.

Kyle looked at the floor, beaten. "Yes, of course I did. Thank you."

"Your brother loves you very much. He also has informed me that you would like to bargain."

Kyle looked up. His eyes were uncertain. "Bargain? Bargain for what?" Kyle asked.

Quick laughed. "Well, I'm not sure. What is it that you want, Kyle? What is it that you asked your brother?"

"I just want Nash to be safe. I want him to live a full life, on Earth, not bothered or tracked by anyone. I don't want him to know what happened here today. I don't want him to know any of this, just live like a normal person. I want him to have a chance to grow old, maybe have kids of his own."

Quick listened, processing what he was told. "I feel there's something else." Quick said.

Kyle shuffled his feet, holding his injured hand. "Nash has nothing left, no family. I'd like you to leave the people of this facility behind so that they can help Nash obtain some of those things. He needs a support system, a family."

"What will you do for me, Kyle?" Quick asked.

"I will do what you want. Kill me if you have to. I can't apologize enough. I just wanted Nash to be safe, that's all. I didn't want him to die or be some sort of experiment. Experiment on me if you'd like. I give up."

"How's the hand?" Quick asked.

Kyle seemed confused and looked down at his hand.

"Uh, it's, well it hurts, a lot," he said.

Quick stepped forward and grasped Kyle's injured hand. He winced from the pain. Just the touch nearly took him to the floor, screaming in pain. Then it stopped, immediately. Kyle looked around and then at Quick. Quick nodded and let go. Kyle looked down at his hand and saw his old self again, no burn, no sign of injury.

"I don't believe it," Kyle said, wiggling his fingers in the air.

"You're a decent man, Kyle, and David looks up to you still. He loves you very much, and most importantly, I trust David."

Kyle wasn't sure what to do and dropped his hands to his sides.

"I will give you a few moments to say goodbye to Nash. We are going to honor your request, Kyle."

Kyle stumbled back a step. "What?"

"Yes. Take a moment, say your goodbyes, then we leave. You will never return here, but you will help us."

Kyle swallowed hard. "Yes, of course."

Quick was gone.

"Kyle?"

"I'm here, Nash."

Kyle held onto Nash by his shoulders. He looked like he had just awakened from a very long night's sleep. He was groggy, but he was back, and looked great to Kyle. He was happy to see his face again. "How do you feel?"

"I feel okay, I guess." Nash continued to look around, trying to remember what they were doing.

"Did I have one of my blackouts? I remember all the people in the next room. Are they still there?"

"Ha! I think I understand your blackout problem now, and yes, they're still there, but I have good news for you."

"Huh? The last thing I remember was you burning your hand." Nash noticed Kyle's hand. He looked at it, then picked it up in his own, turning it every which way, rubbing it, studying it. "Kyle? What happened? I saw your hand. It was hurt. It was hurt bad. How did you?"

Kyle took his hand back and touched Nash's cheek. "Nash, you have to listen to me. There isn't much time."

"Okay, Kyle." Nash was calm, and trusted Kyle. He listened.

Kyle took a deep breath. "This is going to be a lot, so here it goes. The Greys have been with us all along. They followed us here and were planning on taking all of these people, including you."

"They were trapping us here to kill us?" Nash asked nervously, looking around for an escape route.

"Nash? Please listen. There's more."

Nash calmed again, looking desperately at Kyle for answers.

"It's okay. I've made a deal with them," Kyle said.

"What kind of deal, Kyle?"

"I got to talk to my brother."

"David?" Nash said. "How?"

"It's a long story, but please, trust me. Everything is going to be fine. The Greys are going to leave, and they're not taking you or any of the people here at the Dude Ranch. You'll get to stay and grow up with a family of your own. How's that sound?"

Nash couldn't believe it. His eyes lit up again like when they first arrived. "Are you serious?"

"Yes, very serious," Kyle said. He was happy for Nash; he loved that look of innocence in his face.

"That's great, Kyle! This is just great. I can get to know some new friends and you can still come and visit. We can stay in touch. We did it!"

Kyle's smile faded, and he looked at Nash with love in his eyes.

Nash could see that Kyle was holding back. "Kyle? Did I say something wrong?"

"No, of course not, kid. It's just, I may not see you as often as you think. I have to go somewhere else, you know, so we're both safe."

Nash had trouble understanding. He and Kyle were close now. "Where are you going?" Nash asked.

"I have to go with them. I have to go with the Greys."

"Why?" Nash said.

"You have to trust me on this one. It's just the way it is. It's the way it was meant to be."

"I don't understand, Kyle. I thought we were going to try and beat them, you know, run 'em out of town."

Kyle agreed. "Yeah that sounds great, doesn't it? But really, Nash, this whole thing, it's bigger than both of us. We would never be able to tell them not to come here. For all I know, which isn't much, they may have put us here originally."

Nash's expression changed. He didn't like that answer at all. "That's not right, Kyle. What about God? What about God, Kyle? Did you forget about Him?"

"No, of course not, Nash, I didn't. I didn't mean to offend you, but you have to remember that there are a lot of people in the world, and not everyone believes in God. Not everyone believes in aliens. There are actually people who believe nothing. We exist and then we don't . . . lights out, so they say. For all I know, Nash, God made the aliens too and this is some sort of weird way that we interact with them now. Who knows? Maybe in a hundred years we'll all get along better, maybe even coexist on the same planet."

"You're not making any sense, Kyle. Did you bump your head while I was out?"

"No, I'm fine and you're going to be okay, Nash. I've had a great time getting to know you, and I sincerely apologize for the way we met and the way things happened."

"I know now that you feel bad about the past and I accept your apology. Do you really have to go with them, though? I really have enjoyed you too. What am I supposed to do?" Nash asked.

"I promise, kid, they're not going to bother you anymore, it's over. You can live your life any way you see fit and have comfort in knowing that it will honestly be without them. Just remember one thing for me, Nash, and you have to make sure you promise me you'll do it."

"Sure, Kyle, what is it?"

"You have to swear that you'll never speak of them. You have to promise that you'll never tell your story to anyone, no matter what—about anything you've seen or experienced. They'll come after you, Nash. They'll take you away."

"Is that where you're going, Kyle, back to where they come from?"

"I suppose so. I don't know what they'll do to me when I get there, but anymore, I'm tired of fighting it. I'm ready. Besides, it might be a pretty cool ride. Now, did you hear what I said? You have to promise."

"I promise, Kyle. I really do. Never a word."

Kyle hugged Nash. "I'll miss you, kid."

Nash was still fighting the tears, but they kept rolling. "I'll miss you too," he said, sniffling.

Kyle walked toward the front door while Nash watched. He reached out, then paused only inches away from the doorknob. He took a breath, grasped the knob and turned. The door opened with no repercussions and Kyle stood on the front porch.

To either side of him were several Greys, and one in particular gestured for Kyle to take the lead, going toward the open field. Kyle looked up at the sky and could see the craft waiting for him, hovering above the house, hidden above the clouds. As he walked down the steps into the grass, he was greeted by a large figure at least eight feet in height and cloaked in black. The face peered down at him, expressionless. Kyle knew that it was Quick. "Thank you for releasing Nash," Kyle said.

Quick nodded.

The Greys walked Kyle to a specific region in front of the house. Nash was still in the house, watching from the open door, as the Greys stepped away from Kyle, leaving him alone. Nash still cried for Kyle, but felt tremendous joy for him. He knew that Kyle was, in a sense, going home, home to be with David.

Only a few seconds had passed when Nash could hear a low humming sound. He saw Kyle looking around, and the grass around him started to move, then stood straight at attention. Nash raised his hand to wave, catching one last glimpse of Kyle's face.

Kyle disappeared.

30

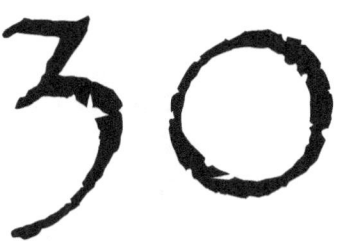

"Sir? Sir? Can you hear me, darlin'?"

Nash opened his eyes. He was looking out the main window in the front office of the Skyward Dude Ranch. He turned around to a large woman with red hair. She had very red lips and bright green eye shadow. He had never seen a woman wear bright colors like that. He remembered that his mother hardly ever wore makeup, but when she did, it was very little. "Where am I?" Nash said.

"You're at the ranch, honey. Do you remember?"

Nash looked out of the window again toward the field. "Who are you?"

"I'm Carolyn. I'm the receptionist here at the Skyward Dude Ranch. Do you remember coming here?"

Nash looked around more and remembered walking in the front door, but he could not recall how he got there. "Yeah. I remember."

He felt something in his hand and looked down. He was holding a pamphlet about the Skyward Dude Ranch. "Did I come alone?"

"No, sir. You walked in with another gentleman, your uncle, and asked me a couple of questions about the ranch. Then you got quiet and walked over to the window after he left.

Nash could see the nervousness in her face. "I'm sorry about that. Uh, may I see the paperwork that my uncle signed?"

"Oh," she began. "Right over here, sugar."

Nash followed her to the front desk and took the papers in his hands. Carolyn's fat index finger found its way over the top of the front page and pointed. "Right here is where he signed, darlin'. You're all set. Would you like to look around? Take the tour? You're official," she said, clapping her chubby little hands together.

Right there in black and white was the one word that brought everything back to Nash. He teared up in an instant and felt nauseous. All of it was a whirlwind, but the strongest feeling of all was the love he had developed for his best friend. That one word jumped off the page straight into his heart.

Kyle.

Carolyn stood behind her desk, waiting for Nash in silence.

He walked over to the front door and took the doorknob in his hand, feeling the cold, hard metal. His feelings for Kyle went out to him and he was okay with the tears that came. He felt happy and realized now all that Kyle had done for him. He was safe now and would have the chance at that new family.

He let go of the doorknob and walked back to the reception desk. Carolyn wasn't sure what to think. Her smile had turned into a look of uncertainty.

"Are there a lot of people who work here?"

"Oh Lord, you scared me. I thought you had changed your mind and were leaving."

Nash wiped away the last tears. "No, I'm going to stay. This is home."

"Oh, that's so sweet. I think I might cry. Well, yes, we do. There is a large staff, even a full kitchen, and one of the best chefs around."

Nash followed as Carolyn began to lead him. She was breaking into her scripted routine for the general tour that most guests probably get.

"Do you have a Sprite?" Nash asked.

Carolyn stopped. "Are you kidding?" she asked, putting her hands on her hips with attitude. "We've got everything, darlin'. Come right this way."

"What about chocolate? Do you have chocolate?"

"Oh Lord, honey, you're going to fit in just fine here."

Nash followed Carolyn on the tour while thoughts of Kyle said hello to him now and then. He was happy.

31

2015

Nash sat on a park bench. The skies were clear, and the breeze that blew through his hair was cool. It was early spring, and the light jacket he wore helped take the sting away from the cold air. It was a gorgeous day; he couldn't have asked for a better one. He watched as kids ran through the park, some playing tag, others on a nearby swing set pushing each other.

He watched the kids play and couldn't help but reminisce about when he was their age, the things he had done, seen, or experienced. He also thought of people who had come in and out of his life. They danced through his mind. One person in particular came to him: Kyle. Kyle had visited Nash several times throughout his life. There had been plenty of times that he could remember asking Kyle for advice while growing up, especially there at the end of his teen years. He felt like Kyle was with him no matter what, and always helped him negotiate through the tough times.

He ended up going to college and earned a degree in education, then found a job back in Crane, Texas, as a history teacher at the local middle school. He enjoyed being around the kids and his job just the same.

After moving back to Crane, he met a girl. They were literally made for each other, and the timing couldn't have been better. She also worked for the school district. Through conversations, while getting to know one another, she told him the story about how she used to pull the night shift at a 7-11. That night seemed so long ago to both of them.

Now, at thirty-nine years of age, he always enjoyed the days he could sit in the park and watch his own son play with the other kids. His son was ten years old and gave Nash a run for his money, always keeping him on his toes. He was, without a doubt, the best part of Nash's life, and Nash didn't hesitate to let people know. At the time of birth, a name had yet to be picked out. Kyle was what Nash insisted upon. He never told his wife the entire story; however, she knew that Kyle had been Nash's best friend before he turned up missing. She agreed that their son should carry on his name.

Kyle jumped off of the swing and ran to his dad. "Daddy!"

Nash leaned forward on the bench, waiting to catch him in his arms. "What's up, buddy?"

Kyle left the ground and landed solid in his dad's arms. They stayed like that, holding one another. Nash closed his eyes and was thankful to have been a dad, to be there for his little boy.

"I love you, Daddy."

"I love you too, son."

Kyle jumped down and started walking back to the playground.

"Hey!" Nash said.

"What?"

"Did I ever tell you why I named you Kyle?"

"No, I thought you just liked the name."

Nash smiled. "Well, I do, but there's another reason also."

"No, you never told me."

"Come on, I want to show you." He took Kyle by the hand and walked back to the car.

About five miles from the park was the cemetery where his friend rested. A couple months after Kyle had disappeared, Nash asked the Skyward Dude Ranch if they would help with the funds of having a plaque put up for Kyle in memorial. That plaque now hung in the crematory section.

"Kyle, this was my friend. His name was Kyle also. He was a very brave man and my best friend."

"Daddy, is he dead?"

Nash, half daydreaming, said, "Yes, son. He's not with us anymore, but he is."

Kyle wrinkled his nose. "Huh? Is he gone or not?"

"I mean, he's always in my heart because he was such a good friend. I think of him from time to time. He helped me out of a difficult situation when I was younger. So, when you were born, I wanted you to have a good strong name. That's why I named you Kyle."

"Oh. Daddy, can we go now? I want to see Mommy."

Nash touched the plaque that was recessed into the wall and spoke to his friend. "I miss you, brother. Thank you so much for the life you've given me. I truly hope you're at peace."

Brother,

In our hearts forever

Kyle Hoffman

December 5, 1948 ~ May 21, 1992

Nash and Kyle walked hand-in-hand back to the car. Nash felt an overwhelming sense of well-being. When they reached the car, Kyle was laughing to himself about something. Nash knew better. This usually meant he was up to something.

"Okay, what's going on? What are you thinking about?"

"I was wondering if we could get some ice cream on the way home," Kyle said.

"Ice cream? You know Mommy would kill us if she knew we ate ice cream before dinner."

Kyle smiled at his dad. "So, does that mean we're gonna do it?"

"You definitely took after me, kid. Let's go get some ice cream."

Kyle started jumping around. "Yea!" He looked at his dad before getting in the car. "I love you, Daddy."

Nash knelt down and looked into Kyle's eyes. "I love you, too, and don't you ever forget it."

Kyle smiled. At that moment, Nash caught a glimpse of something in his son's eyes that he couldn't put his finger on. Was it a light, a reflection from behind, or his mind playing tricks on him? Whatever it was he saw in his son's eye that day, he let it go and chocked it up to pure coincidence.

About the Author:

Matthew Gene lives in Aledo, Texas with his wife Kim, and their two kids. He is also the author of the sci-fi/fantasy novella, Hope.